THE SISTER WIFE'S HUSBAND

ANYA MORA

THE SISTER WIFE'S HUSBAND

A GRAY WEST MYSTERY BOOK 3

By Anya Mora

My husband has always been dangerous.
But I never thought he was a killer.
One phone message changes everything.
The cult where I spent fifteen years of my life is preparing for the unthinkable.
My son has returned to the fold.
I must find him before it is too late.
But it's not just his life that's at stake—it's the entire congregation of Garden Temple.
I thought I was destined to be a sister wife and mother, but it turns out I am so much more.
I am a woman who must stop her husband's madness before he does something irreversible.

I must stop him before it's too late.

The Sister Wife's Husband is book three is a new suspense series.

1

THE BEDROOM SPINS around me as my fingers grip my son's phone.

I replay the message. "Abel, I know you're still looking for Ruthie." Bethany's voice is withdrawn, distant. "But I really hope you can make it back to Garden Temple soon because the prophet has told us his revelation. We've been waiting for so many years for this time, for this moment, but it's here. Our garden has grown and it's time. It's time for all of us to return to Eden."

I close the flip phone that Olive took from her big brother's backpack before he slipped away in the night. Bethany's words linger heavy in the air. Did someone pressure her to make this call, or was it something she wanted to do? A warning?

"I have to go get him," I whisper, sitting on the edge my bed, still in my pajamas, my hair unruly, my heart heavy. One night of peaceful sleep was all the rest I was getting. Ruthie, my eight-year-old, spent two nights in captivity, and she was just found. Now my son, Abel, a teenager with nothing but reckless love on his mind, is gone. Is he trying to spare me more pain?

"What's going on?" Ruthie asks, rubbing her eyes, now awake.

"Abel left," I tell her, pushing her wavy hair from her eyes. "He left for Bethany."

"Is he coming back with her? With their baby?" she asks.

Baby. Bethany is fifteen and pregnant with my son's child. Everything about this situation feels like history repeating itself, except it is so much worse this time. I need to get them both out before something irreversible happens.

I look at Olive. At twelve, she understands that Abel and Bethany leaving the compound, where they've lived their entire lives, is no simple thing. It would mean turning away from their family and friends, and if they believe the prophet's words, they might refuse to come with me at all.

"I can't wait to find out what either of them are planning," I tell both my girls. "I'm scared something bad might happen to them if I don't go get them and force them to leave myself."

"Something bad like what?" Ruthie asks, following me as I get out of bed.

"Bad like Dad might never let them leave," Olive says. But in my gut I know it is worse than that. Worse than not letting them leave. Going to Eden means moving into the place Jeremiah has prepared for us.

But what if he has sinister plans once they get there? What if it's not a destination so much as a spiritual state of mind? A permanent state.

"We can call the police," Ruthie says. "They are super nice. They helped you find me, didn't they?"

The three of us descend the stairs, entering the kitchen. The house feels empty without my son here even though he'd only been here a few days.

The police have been in my house for the last two days as we worked tirelessly to find Ruthie. The idea of calling them again exhausts me, but I know I need help if I'm going to do this.

"The police in Tacoma aren't the same police who live near the compound; they're different departments," I explain to Olive and Ruthie as I begin to make a pot of coffee. Coffee. I feel like it's all I live on.

"What do you mean?" Olive asks. "I thought the police would help anybody."

"Right," I say, "but when we suspected your father of being the one who took Ruthie, the police from Tacoma were the ones who drove over to interview him and to clear him, not the police who work where he lives. Does that make sense?"

"Kind of," Ruthie says slowly. "So you're saying we need the police by the compound to help get Abel back?" Her voice lifts as she finishes her sentence, still too young to fully understand this, and honestly, I'm not sure if I want her to.

I need to protect her. God knows I haven't done a very good job of it so far, considering she was stolen from our driveway while taking out the trash.

"So you have to go to the compound and then ask the police for help once you get there?" Olive asks.

"I think so," I tell her.

If I drive to Grant County, I can go to the

police station and explain what I think is going to happen at the compound. It's not that I fear Jeremiah is going to convince the entire congregation at Garden Temple to drink the not-so-metaphorical Kool-Aid and take their lives, but that I don't know where Eden is. It's a secret location only the men are privy to. If Jeremiah is taking them there in the hopes of fulfilling the prophecy he's been preaching about for two decades, I need to know where that is exactly.

Why didn't I ask Abel more questions when he was here? Get an address for the work site at least? But I know why I didn't. When Abel was here for those few days, we were consumed with looking for Ruthie.

"Maybe you should call Boone," Olive says as she pulls out a jug of milk from the refrigerator.

Boone.

I consider him, knowing Boone is one person I do feel safe with. Talking to a detective might help me get some clarity, and to be honest, I could use that.

"That's not a terrible idea," I say, biting my bottom lip.

"Is he your friend, like Patrick was your friend?" Ruthie asks me.

Patrick was another man I was friendly with, but Patrick used me, put me in danger so he could get closer to his own desires. He lured me in by paying for my Ruthie's dance lessons and helping me with the grocery bills. I thought he was a friend, but he wasn't, and now it doesn't even matter. Patrick was killed because of his dangerous decisions, the schemes he pulled me into, endangering me in the process.

"No, Boone is nothing like Patrick," I tell her. "Patrick was what they call a wolf in sheep's clothing."

"He seemed nice on the outside, but inside he had really sharp teeth?" Ruthie asks.

"Exactly," I tell her.

"And Boone," Olive says, "doesn't bite. He's more like a gentle lion."

"Yeah." Ruthie grins. "He even has kind of reddish hair, like a lion's mane."

I smile despite myself. "Yeah, I suppose he does."

"So call him," Olive says, shoving my phone across the kitchen counter. "He'll know how to help you."

"I'm sure he has work," I say.

"Yeah, but I have a feeling he'd do anything for you, Mom."

"Why do you say that?"

Olive widens her eyes, rolls them. "Mom, I may be twelve, but I know a thing or two about crushes."

I snort. "Do you now?" Talking about crushes seems absurd considering the situation, but I don't want the girls to sense my worry. I want them to believe everything is fine. That this is just a little hiccup in getting their brother home. So I indulge them with this conversation.

"Yeah," Olive says, "Boone likes you."

I shake my head. "Olive, it's not like that."

Ruthie and Olive share a look I have never seen them share before, a look that says, "Oh my God, Mom likes him too."

Do I?

"Regardless of my feelings or Boone's feelings," I say, "there are bigger things to worry about right now than crushes."

Olive opens her mouth wide. "So you do have a crush on Boone?"

"No," I say. "Olive." I shake my head. "Honey, please don't say that."

"Why?" Olive says. "You should be happy. Your whole life has basically sucked."

"That's not true," I say, defensive. "My

whole life has been happy because you've been in it."

"That's nice and all, Mom, but you're not just a mother, you know? You're also a person. So maybe your life as a mom has been good. But what about your life as Grace?"

I turn away from her, reaching for the cream to pour into my black coffee, not wanting her to see my face. Her question is like a gut punch and a sliver of hope all at once. She isn't wrong.

My life *as a person* has sucked.

I take a drink of my coffee, turning to face my girls again. They're cutting into a quiche that someone left at our house. The fridge is stocked with food from well-meaning neighbors. No one wanted us to worry about something as trivial as meals when we were looking for Ruthie. I'm grateful, and always will be, for the people who have circled around us in our time of need.

I hate that I'm going to have to ask them for more help now.

"I think I'll call him," I say. The girls smile. "*Not* because of a crush, but because he is a detective, so he'll know what to do."

"I don't know why it's so dangerous just to go and ask Abel to come back here with you,"

Ruthie says. "Why are you so worried about it, Mom?"

I swallow, not wanting my little girl to understand the depth of the worry I have in my heart. Not just for Abel and Bethany and the child growing in her womb, but for my sister wives, Naomi and Lydia, and all their children, the little ones I helped raise. And all the other mothers and fathers and growing kids at the compound, hundreds of lives so intricately wrapped around Jeremiah's. A man who has intentions that aren't pure in the least. But they're so blinded by their devotion, they don't see it like that.

There is so much more at stake than Abel coming home with the girl he loves at his side. Getting them here safely, and stopping Jeremiah before he does something irreversible is all that matters. The way he stormed out of this house two days ago is fresh in my mind. He was livid. With me.

Bethany's voice mail made it clear what they were doing. "It's time to harvest what we've planted." Her voice from the message echoes in my mind. "It's time to go to Eden."

I reach for my phone with coffee in my other hand. "I'm just going to go into the living room," I tell them. Ruthie jumps over to a basket by the back door filled with library books that I've gotten at my job. I watch as she pulls out a *Dog Man* comic and carries it back to the kitchen table. The sisters open it up and begin laughing, reading the frames as they eat their quiche.

In the living room, I turn on the heat. It's cold in here, and I curl up in an armchair with a blanket over my knees. The bone-chilling coldness from the snow this weekend has settled in around us, and I realize with a start that the girls should have been in school today. It's a Monday. It was the last thing on my mind.

Ruthie was just found. We still need to recover.

I run my hands over my eyes knowing there's no time for that now. I've got to get across the mountains and to the compound before it's too late.

Before calling Boone, though, I try the house phone, knowing if Lydia and Naomi are there, one of them will pick up. It rings and rings and rings. No answer.

Frustrated, I call Boone, and thankfully he answers right away.

"Gray?" he asks. "Is everything okay?" There's worry in his voice.

"Well," I tell him, exhaling. "Not exactly."

"Is it Ruthie?" His voice is raised in alarm.

"No, no, she's here. She and Olive are eating breakfast in the kitchen."

"Then what is it?" he asks, knowing me well enough by now to know something is on my mind. Something that isn't good.

"It's Abel," I tell him, "he's gone."

"Oh shit," he says.

"Yeah, but it's more than that, Boone."

"What do you mean, more than that?"

"Are you working today?" I ask, cutting to the chase.

"I have the next few days off," he tells me. "Why? Do you need me to come over?"

"Actually, I was wondering if you could come with me," I say. "Come with me to get my son."

2

BOONE TELLS me he'll be here in ninety minutes, which works out well. It'll give me enough time to figure out what I'm supposed to do with my daughters.

I'm not bringing them back to the compound *ever*, especially not now, considering the situation that's unfolding.

Part of me wanted to hash it all out with Boone right there on the phone, explain to him what I believe Jeremiah is plotting, and run my fears past him.

But in my gut, I know what I need to do. And I've got to start trusting myself. My intuition is one of my greatest assets, and for far too many years I haven't taken heed of it. That ends now.

I'm going to Eastern Washington, whether or not Boone comes with me.

Thankfully he agreed to come, he knows how urgent this is. He's heard my testimony about Jeremiah. He knows some of the pieces to the puzzle of my heart.

I think of my neighbors, knowing they would do anything for me. They've been committed and devoted friends the last few weeks. Besides, last night when Sophie was saying goodbye to the girls, she told them she was always up for a sleepover.

I dial Luna's number, knowing the girls will feel safest with her. They've spent time at her house; they adore her oldest daughter, Sophie, and her husband, Hank, is a good man, a doctor.

"Hey," Luna says. "I wasn't expecting to hear from you, but it's nice."

"Is this a good time?"

"Yeah, it's great. I just got out of yoga. It was incredible. You should really come with me. There's this new studio down on Fourteenth. The instructor is on fire."

"That sounds great," I say, having never done yoga in my entire life, "but I was actually calling to ask you something."

"What?" Luna asks. "Sorry, it's kind of loud

in here. I'm grabbing a coffee. Give me a sec. I'll call you right back." She hangs up and I rethink everything. Maybe this is a terrible idea, having the girls go somewhere right after Ruthie was found. But the thought of taking them with me into danger is even more unbearable.

I pour a second cup of coffee, give the girls a smile, and tell them Boone is coming over.

"Really?" Olive says. "That's awesome. See? He'll know what to do."

I nod. "I made a decision. I'm going to the compound," I tell them. "I need to. I will never be able to forgive myself if I don't go and try to get your brother to come home."

Olive's eyes lift. "We're going back?"

I shake my head. "Not we. Me. You're saying here. You're going to miss school today, but tomorrow you need to go back, so I'm going to ask one of the neighbors if you can stay with them."

"Neighbors?" Ruthie says, her eyes widening.

"Not him," I say. "He is never coming back," I promise, thinking of Granger, the man down the street who kept my daughter captive for two days. "He is going to be in jail for the rest of his life, Ruthie. But I don't think it's a good idea for you to come to the compound. They're not making very safe decisions there right now, and my first priority is making sure you are both out of harm's way."

Olive nods. "I get it," she says. "I mean, part of me wants to come because I miss Naomi and I want to see her baby, but I also trust that you know what you're doing."

Those words give me more confidence than Olive may ever know. She trusts me. She trusts that I will make sound and good and well-intentioned decisions. She trusts me with her life.

"Thank you," I say. "It's not my first choice either, but ..."

"It's okay, Mom," Ruthie says. "Maybe I can have that sleepover with Sophie!"

My phone rings and I hold up a finger. "Hold that thought, okay?" The girls return to their comic book and I answer the phone. "Luna?"

"Hey," she says brightly. "Sorry, I didn't realize there was such a long line at North Side. That place is amazing."

"Yeah," I say. "It's great."

"So what did you want to ask?" Luna asks warmly.

"I was actually wondering if ... and look, I

understand this is totally an imposition, but I need to go to Eastern Washington. Today."

"Oh no, what's happened?" she asks.

"It's Abel," I tell her. "He went back to his father's, and he's a really dangerous man. Abel thinks he's protecting his girlfriend by going, but I'm afraid he might do more harm than good."

"I didn't realize he had a girlfriend back home."

"That's not his home," I say. "Where his father lives is ... My house is going to be his home," I tell her, "but he doesn't quite see it like that yet."

"Young love?"

"Kind of," I tell her, not wanting to say it all —that my son and the girl he loves are caught up in the cult where they've been raised and that Bethany, the girl he impregnated, is set to marry Abel's father at the end of the week. That might be a little bit of an overshare, a little more than Luna can wrap her mind around before she's finished her morning latte.

"Look," I say, "I know things have been chaotic with me and my family, and Ruthie just came home, but I'm really scared for Abel. And I'm scared if I don't go right now and get him, I might never have the chance. He's reckless and he's emotional and ..."

Luna cuts me off. "It's okay," she says. "I don't understand all of it, but I saw your interview. I've heard some whisperings about your ex showing up at your place so I get it, kind of. But more than anything, I trust you, Gray. I know you wouldn't be asking this unless you really needed it."

"Thank you," I say, exhaling, tears in my eyes. "Boone is on his way over, and he offered to go with me, so I don't have to travel by myself, but I think it would be safer for the girls to not see their father."

"Absolutely," Luna says. "I'm on my way home right now, and then I'll come over and get them, okay?"

"Okay," I say. "Thank you."

In the kitchen, I explain to the girls what's going on. That they're going to have a few days at Luna's house.

"Really?" Olive beams. "That's awesome. I've never had a sleepover in the real world."

I laugh. "Oh my goodness. Is that what we're calling it, the real world versus..."

She shrugs. "The cult? Yeah, basically."

"When did you get so grown-up?" I ask her.

She bites her bottom lip. "I'm not sure you want me to answer that."

I'm not sure either, hating the life my children have had to lead because of where they were born and raised.

"Let's get you packed up," I say.

Ruthie jumps off her stool. "This is going to be awesome. I love playing at Luna's house."

"Good," I say, wanting her to be happy and safe. Desperate to protect her from anything bad happening to her again. It's naïve, of course, that longing to protect the girls' innocence when so much of it has already been taken, but it's still something I hold on to. I can't do everything for them, but I can do my best to make sure they're safe.

And I will with all the fight I have in me.

Soon, Luna's here, and she's giving me a big warm hug and a latte. "I know, you've probably already had coffee, but I swung back into the shop and grabbed you one because it's just that good. I promise."

I take a sip. "Thank you. You really didn't have to."

"I know I didn't have to, but hey, what are friends for?" She shrugs and gives me a smile. Then looking over at my girls, she claps her hands. "So, I already texted the neighbors, and everyone is all set. We're going to have a Monday night pizza party," she says, lifting her eyebrows. "How does that sound? We're going to get some pizza. The kids are going to watch a movie. It's going to be awesome."

"Cool," Olive says. "Mom helped us pack, so we've got all of our stuff ready."

"We're all set, then," Luna says, giving them a big smile. "I am so excited for this. And the best part, Sophie is in school today, which means we have the whole day to do something epic. I heard there is a new trampoline park. Have you ever ..."

Ruthie starts jumping up and down. "Really? The indoor one with, like, a hundred trampolines in it?"

"Yeah, Tomas told me about it. Sounds really cool." Olive grins.

"Okay, great," Luna says, "I thought if we're already playing hooky, we might as well have a blast at it."

I give her the biggest smile, relief flooding my body. Luna recognizes how intense this situation is. And instead of letting the girls feel any of that, she is wiping it away with pure distraction. Luna is more than a good mom. She's a smart one too.

I kiss the girls goodbye, telling them I love

them over and over and over again. Eventually, Olive takes my hands and says, "Mom, we got it. We'll call you tonight, okay? Before we go to bed."

"Okay," I say. "And tell Luna if you need anything, right?"

"Of course," Luna. "Anything at all. Don't be worried or hesitant. And I have a guest room, so you girls can share a bed in there, and it'll be great. I'll even take you to school in the morning."

"We don't have to ride the bus?" Olive says.

"Guess not," Luna says with another smile. "Okay, one last hug, and then we need to go. We've got to get to the trampoline park before all the moms with toddlers get there."

The girls smile. "Love you, Mom."

"Love you more," I say, watching them go. They jump down the porch, headed to the sidewalk to walk to Luna's house. Luna gives me a final hug.

"Hey," she says, "you got this. You're seriously the strongest woman I've ever met, so I have no doubt in your abilities. Go get your son, and tell him to get his punk ass home."

"Okay," I say, laughing somehow.

"And get dressed," she adds. "If Boone's

taking you on a road trip, I feel like there might be some implication there."

"Stop," I groan.

She shrugs. "I don't know. I mean, there is a connection." Boone's car is pulling up. "Oh my God, you haven't even dressed yet and he's here. What's he going to think?"

I shove her off the porch. "Luna, enough," I say with a laugh. "Seriously, it's nothing."

Luna rolls her eyes. "Right, nothing but a handsome detective driving you across the state. And you're probably going to have to stay at a hotel together, right? At least for a night, maybe two, maybe three." She lets out a slight whimper, and I turn red in the face.

"Luna, stop!"

She shrugs. "All right. But life is hard, girl. Have a little fun when you can." She gives Boone a wave as she passes him on the sidewalk, and my shoulders fall for the first time in forever. Hope. That's what this feels like, hope.

Maybe I really can go to Eastern Washington and get Abel and Bethany and bring them home, and we can all be happy, together.

Maybe.

And right now, a maybe feels like a better bet than a no.

3

"SORRY," I say once Boone enters the house, "I hadn't had a chance to get ready yet. I was busy getting the girls out the door."

He shakes his head. "No, don't worry about it," he says. "I'm not in a rush."

"Well, I kind of am," I tell him honestly. "Abel's freaking me out."

"Do you want to talk about it now? Or when we get on the road?"

"On the road. I'm going to go change real quick, and then we can head out. Help yourself to coffee in the kitchen."

He smiles. "There's always coffee on in this house. And in your hand." He points to the latte Luna brought me.

"Is it different at yours?" I ask, having never

been to his cabin in Buckley, though he's told me about it.

"I reckon it is."

"You *reckon*? Wow. One night back in the country, and you start sounding like a mountain man."

He snorts. "Is that what you think?"

"I don't know what to think," I say honestly. "I've only ever seen you in my house or in your car or at the police station, though we did get coffee at that coffee shop once."

"The coffee that tasted like soap."

"It was a lavender latte," I say, pleased that he remembers. "Okay, I'm going to go upstairs and get dressed, and I'll be back in a few."

"Great, I'm going to make a few calls anyway. I promised Charlie I'd ..." He stops mid-sentence.

"Promised Charlie what?" I ask him to finish.

"Follow up," he says. "She kind of collected some information about your children's father."

I nod slowly. "Yeah? What did she find?"

"It's not good," he says.

"More to talk about in the car?" I ask, a lilt to my voice.

"Yeah," he says, "more stuff to talk about in

the car."

Upstairs, I grab some clothes from my dresser drawers. Jeans, a few sweaters, socks, and underwear, Luna's words echoing in my mind. *You might be sharing a hotel room together.*

It's ridiculous. I'm not going to sleep in a room with Boone. Though, actually, I might. I have no idea what's going to happen when we get to Moses Lake. I'm hoping it will be an easy situation, but nothing with Jeremiah is ever simple.

Besides, I don't exactly have lacy bras and lingerie to shove into my overnight bag just in case something happens with this divorced cop, who is completely out of my league.

Instead of my granny nightgown, I pull out a pair of sweats and a tank top, knowing at least they flatter my figure a bit. *Flatter my figure?* When have I ever thought like this in my life?

In the bathroom, I pack a small zippered pouch with my toothbrush and face wash. I don't have a traditional toiletries bag or luggage. I've never gone on vacation anywhere, never had to pack anything, not like this. When I left Garden Temple, I threw the things I owned in a few garbage bags and made a run for it. This so much different.

I find a tote bag from the library and fill it

with my things, adding a hairbrush, a jean jacket. After, I swipe some mascara over my eyelashes and concealer on my cheeks, some sheer lipstick on my lips and add it all to the pouch, placing it in the tote bag. I smooth my hair down with my hands before tucking it behind my ears. I look fine. Fine enough to confront my husband—or whatever he is to me now—and hopefully stop him from doing something horrible.

I'm dreading the car ride because I know I will have to explain all of this to Boone. Tell him things that he might not be at all prepared to hear.

Downstairs, I find him washing the dishes from the girls' breakfast.

"You didn't have to do that," I tell him.

He shrugs, turning off the tap and drying his hands on a towel. "I know." He looks up at me. "You look nice."

"Thanks," I say, looking him over for the first time today. He has on a green flannel shirt, dark blue jeans, brown boots. He's got a canvas jacket slung over the dining room chair. His hair curls at the ends. His beard is scruffy, and I like that.

"What?" he asks.

"Nothing," I say, suddenly nervous,

embarrassed.

"Okay," he says, "you ready?"

I nod. "Yeah. What about your dog, Matisse? Where's he going?"

Boone says, "I dropped him off at my sister's. Remember her? You guys met once at the brewery."

I laugh. "Is that what we're calling that? I thought I ran away mortified that you were on a date and I'd caught you with another woman."

"Another woman," he says. "That kind of implies that there is a woman." My cheeks turn bright red. "Hey," Boone says. "We're good. Aren't we?"

I nod. "I think so."

"Okay," he says. "Anyway, I took Matisse to my sister's. She's good with him being there until we come back. I told her it might be a few days, that sound about right?"

"Yeah. And Luna's good with the girls as long as necessary. She seems to understand the situation."

"Good," he says. "And not to be intense, but I told Charlie to get a guy to patrol the neighborhood."

"My neighborhood?" I ask.

"Yeah. Your neighborhood. After the last

two days with Ruthie, I don't want anything to happen." He runs his hand over his jaw. "Leaving your girls bothers me too."

I nod. "I can't have them come. I'm not sure what the situation is going to be like at the compound and—"

Boone cuts me off. "I know," he says. "And after I read the file from Charlie , I feel like it might be more grim than I've prepared myself for."

I swallow. "Right. So, you still want to do this?"

He nods. "Yeah. And I'm driving. Your car is a piece of crap: no offense."

"None taken."

He takes my tote bag from me, and I lock up my house, keeping my porch light on. He adds my bag to his trunk, and I see he has a compact suitcase already in it.

He doesn't open the door for me and I'm relieved. That would feel too much like a date. In the car, Boone's classical music begins to play, and I smile, remembering it's his favorite.

"So," he says as we begin to drive out of town, "you talk."

"All right," I say, and I begin to explain my story as we leave Tacoma and get on the freeway: I-5 to I-90, and then farther still. We need to get over the mountains and get to Moses Lake. It's going to be a five-hour drive, plenty of time to explain the situation. I want Boone to have a good idea of what we're walking into before we actually walk into it.

"Well, I'm going to start with the end," I tell him.

"Abel leaving Tacoma," Boone says, looking over at me.

"Right. But the reason he left is because of Bethany."

"His girlfriend?" Boone fills in.

"Right. She's pregnant and—"

"Oh wow," Boone says, "I didn't realize."

"We just found out."

Boone shrugs. "So is that the deal? He went back because he wants to be with his girlfriend?"

I shake my head. "No, he went back because of the phone call Bethany made last night, telling him the time was now; the end was near. That the garden was ready to harvest."

"What does that mean?" Boone asks.

I swallow, not wanting to hold any of this back.

"It means wherever it is they are going, they won't be coming back."

4

"WHERE WOULD THEY GO, EXACTLY?" Boone asks, his eyes on the road.

I swallow. "I know they were building a place called Eden. Jeremiah preached about it for years, this place the men were preparing for us, but the women didn't know where it was."

"Is there more to it than that?" Boone asks.

"Look, I'm not someone who's prone to exaggeration," I tell him. "I'm a no-nonsense kind of person. I never look to create drama. But I'm scared Eden might be more than a physical place. It might be permanent ... like ... death?"

"That's a big claim," Boone says. "Do you have reason to believe Jeremiah might be planning on doing something drastic?"

"Nothing beyond a feeling," I say. "I don't know how to proceed. That's why I called you. The situation with Jeremiah is not just an abusive ex who won't leave me alone. He's more than that, he's my ..." I bite my bottom lip, trying to find the word for it. "For a long time, he was my whole world. When I mentioned the compound where we lived with the kids, it wasn't just a housing development or a group of hippies living on a plot of land. I'm not sure what Charlie's file told you about Jeremiah, but his compound is where his congregation lives, where his followers worship. Garden Temple isn't just a church, it's a way of life. It's a belief system. There are hundreds of people who are committed to anything and everything Jeremiah says. He's more than a preacher, Boone. He's their prophet."

Boone tenses, and I reach for the heater blasting warm air because a chill has taken over me, over us.

"That is pretty much what Charlie found out," Boone says. "You were in a cult, and when you escaped to Tacoma, it was your chance to save your daughters."

"Basically, yeah, I was in a cult," I admit. "I didn't have words for it then. Not really. After my parents died, I was put in the care of my aunt and uncle, and they had just gotten to know Jeremiah. They had been a part of his church before it moved to the compound. They were early followers. Back then it wasn't like it is now."

"And what is it like now?"

"Now, it's dangerous. I'm scared for the children there, for my sister wives and ..."

"Sister wives," Boone repeats, frowning, "what do you mean?"

"I wasn't Jeremiah's only partner. He had two other wives, Lydia and Naomi, and they had children with him too. I was Jeremiah's first wife and ..."

Boone exhales. "Damn, Gray, this is a hell of a lot."

"I know. I told you I was complicated. If this is too much, I ..."

"No, it's not too much. I'm just trying to process the person I know you to be and the story you're telling me of where you've been. Damn, I thought you were strong before, but ..."

"What? Now you think I'm crazy?"

"No," Boone says, "anything but. Now I think you're a hell of a lot braver than I ever knew."

"Leaving was the hardest thing I ever did," I

tell him, never having admitted this to anyone. "I was bound to Jeremiah when I was fourteen years old, and he was twice my age. I gave birth to Abel when I was fifteen. I knew the future Olive would have. She was growing up so fast, and Jeremiah had a husband in mind for her, and I couldn't bear it. Even though I was terrified of what Jeremiah might do if I got caught leaving with the girls, I was more scared of what would happen to them if I never tried. I wouldn't be able to live with myself."

"And Abel, why didn't he come with you?"

"Abel has always had a connection to his father that was different than his connection to me. I knew if I told Abel I was running, he would tell Jeremiah, and they would stop me." I blink back tears. Boone notices and reaches for my hand.

"Hey, it's okay. You don't have to tell me all of this if you don't want to."

"No, I need you to know what you're walking into because the situation is incredibly twisted."

"I'm starting to understand that."

"Jeremiah's really mad right now. With me gone, he's taking it out on Abel."

"How?" Boone asks.

"Jeremiah said he was going to marry

Bethany, the girl that Abel has been in love with since forever. The girl who's apparently pregnant with Abel's child."

Boone draws in a sharp breath. "Shit."

"Yeah. It's messed up. When Abel came home a few nights ago, it was with the hope of me helping him get Bethany out. But then Ruthie was taken. And now ... now it's different."

"Can I hear the message?" he asks.

"Of course." I pull Abel's flip phone out of my purse and I press play. Bethany's message fills the car.

The time has come. The end is near. It's ready for harvest. When the message ends, I turn the phone over in my hands.

"I'm not a sensationalist, but this message," I whisper, "it's pretty damn sensational."

"I agree," Boone says. "It's terrifying."

"That's why we have to go. Jeremiah knows that I'm not scared of him anymore. He knows that I'm comfortable around law enforcement. And so, despite whatever hold he thought he had over me, when he showed up at my house two days ago, he realized his power was gone. And without control over me, he knew I would tell his secrets, expose him for what he is. A child molester, a fraud, a zealot. That's why he is taking the entire congregation and going into hiding. He knows that his time is over, that his reign is done."

"The first wife running away couldn't have been good for his image," Boone sums up. "If his son escaped with his next wife, he'd really take a hit. He's ending it all to save face." Boone clears his throat. "You really think they'll go completely off the grid?" Boone asks.

"Jeremiah doesn't do anything halfway. But it could mean a few things—going to the physical location that they were building, or connecting to the divine, being one with our Creator."

"Hell, Gray. I'm glad you called me. I wouldn't want you to do this alone."

"When we get to Moses Lake, maybe we should go to the police first; tell them everything."

Boone shakes his head. "Before that, how about we go to the compound? See if a simple conversation might stop things before they get out of hand? Gray, I know you haven't lived in the real world long, but this could end up like Ruby Ridge, like Waco, something really bad."

"I know," I say. "I want to avoid that. There are people that follow Jeremiah that I love, that my children love. Hell, Abel is there. I don't want someone to call in the feds, and suddenly the whole compound is blown up. I want the people I care about safe."

Boone nods in understanding, his foot on the gas, and I see his speed increase. He wants to get over these mountains and to the compound as quickly as I do.

Now he understands that time is truly running out.

5

THE TIRES on Boone's car crunch as we roll onto the gravel drive of the compound. The earth is flat and dusty, brown. The buildings in the distance made up my life, my whole world, for so long.

"This is it," I tell him. "This is Garden Temple."

It's cold out. I can see my breath in the air. We made good time, only stopping for lunch, and now it's midafternoon. I think of the girls at Luna's. Sophie's probably getting off school, and Olive and Ruthie are probably bouncing up and down in excitement to hang out with the coolest teenager they've ever met. I know they're safe though, so I don't need to worry about them right now. Right now, I need to focus on Abel.

"Do many of the members of the church have cars?" Boone asks.

I twist my lips. "Sure, I mean, the men do, and the women would drive them sometimes. We'd go to Walmart for groceries every once in a while, at least the more trusted women."

"Where you one of the trusted women?"

I nod. "Yes. I was the prophet's first wife. I had a very high-ranking position."

"And your other sister wives?"

"Lydia was Jeremiah's second wife, and she was always jealous. I think since the day I met her, she was unhappy. She always wanted more, and I used to be so frustrated by it," I tell him as we drive closer to the buildings, "but as I got older, I realized I didn't need to be angry about her jealousy. She deserved a husband who loved her with his whole heart, not a portion of it. It makes me sad," I tell Boone. "Thinking about how much Lydia deserved and never got."

"She might get it still," Boone says.

"Maybe," I say, "but when you believe something with all you've got, it's very difficult to let go of it."

"You did, though, right?" Boone asks. "You don't still believe what Jeremiah preaches, do you?"

"No," I say, "I gave that up long before I actually left the church. But I had ten years living with my parents, having a really strong idea of what a healthy and happy childhood could mean. What loving parents looked like. Lydia didn't. She grew up in this world; it's all she's ever known. Before her family moved to Garden Temple, they were going to Jeremiah's church. She was raised in a very conservative situation."

"And Jeremiah's third wife?"

I smile. "Naomi. Now she's the wild card. His youngest and most fertile wife. She had four kids in as many years."

Boone coughs at that.

"Sorry," I say, "it's a fact. We all slept with Jeremiah."

"I know. I just hate thinking about that."

I press my lips together. "Yeah, I hate thinking about it too." I point straight ahead. "There, that's the church where we'd meet, and next to it, that brown building, that's the supply outpost where we would have our shared resources, pantry items, clothing, et cetera. The green building to the left, that's the school-house, and the rest of the buildings are the homes."

"They don't look like houses," he says.

I shake my head. "No, Jeremiah always had this big vision for what the compound would look like. I think he wanted it to be much grander than it ever was. Money was always an issue."

"Still, how did you guys survive? Pay your bills, keep the lights on?"

"When you joined the church, you had to hand your assets over to prove you were fully committed to the message. So there was a lot of property that could be sold. People's retirement funds and houses and any sorts of assets were sold, and the money was given to the church. That helped greatly. And the men also had a construction company, so they would do roofing and other building jobs around the community."

"If they were construction workers, you'd think they would have made this place a little nicer."

I know what he's seeing, cinder-block foun-dations and exposed siding, half-finished boxes with simple roofs, porches made from plywood. Wood crates standing in as steps.

"This house," I tell him, pointing to the white one to the right, "that's where I lived."

Boone stops his car. "It doesn't look like there's anybody here."

"I know," I say, swallowing my fear. The place looks like a ghost town, empty. There are only a few cars parked in front of the houses, but no children are out playing, no men jumping in trucks and heading to a work site. It's quiet. Too quiet.

We get out of the car, and Boone places a hand on my shoulder. "I'm right here. I'm not going anywhere."

"Thank you," I tell him.

I knock on the door, something I've never done in my life. This was my house. I remember moving into it.

"When Jeremiah and I got married, we lived in a small room in the back of the church because he'd never planned on taking a wife," I tell Boone, "but once I was pregnant with Abel, we knew we needed a home, so this one was built for us. Later, it became the home for our whole family after Lydia and Naomi joined us."

Boone runs a hand over his jaw. "No one's answering."

"I'm scared," I say, my voice quiet. "What if they've already ..."

"Hey, if they've already done something irreversible, then you did everything you could have. You're here, aren't you? You came as fast as you could."

"I know, but ..."

"We're breaking the law, but I don't care. Open the door, Gray."

I close my eyes, my fingers on the knob, and I push it open. The door creaks, but there's no other sound. I step into the hallway, my feet on the linoleum floor. "Hello?" I call out. "Lydia? Naomi? It's me, Grace."

There's no sound of children's feet bounding down the hall to see who's here to visit. No smells of dinner cooking on the stove. Nothing at all.

"I should look in the bedrooms," I say. "Come with me?"

He nods, and we climb the stairs. I press open the door of the children's room first. My heart is tight in my chest, terrified of seeing the worst. But the rows of bunk beds are empty, unmade with rumpled sheets. The fact that they are not filled is the most beautiful thing I've ever seen.

"I was so scared," I tell Boone, gasping. "That they'd ..."

"I know," he says. "I know."

We walk down the hall. All the doors are open, and not a single soul is here. No corpses to be found. Boone places a hand on my shoulder, and I like how close he is. Not letting me out of his sight.

"Would they have gone somewhere else to do this? The church?" Boone asks.

"Lydia's and Naomi's rooms, maybe?" Fear wraps itself up in my throat as I step into Lydia's empty bedroom, seeing a vase with fake flowers on her dresser, a water glass on her nightstand. I pull open her closet, and I don't know what I was expecting to see, but there is nothing of note. Naomi's room is the same. An empty bassinet sits next to her bed for her newest baby.

"Where was your room?" he asks me.

"Downstairs in the back of the house, closer to Jeremiah's."

"I bet your sister wives hated that."

"Oh, they did," I say.

We walk through the living room. I try to see the furniture through Boone's eyes. Leftovers from thrift stores, random items that members of the congregation brought with them when they moved in. There is a large dining room table with more than a dozen chairs circling it, a kitchen with two refrigerators and two stoves side by side.

"You guys were cooking for an army."

I smile. "Yeah, Jeremiah had a big family."

"Do you miss it?" he asks. "This place?"

"I miss moments," I tell Boone honestly as I step into my bedroom. It's exactly as I left it. "I miss the big family dinners. And birthdays, because even though we didn't celebrate them, us moms still knew it was a special day when our little ones came into the world. We weren't supposed to give presents or anything, but we would still do nice things for the children, bake them their favorite cookies, sew them a new outfit. Those days were special. I miss how full life felt here with sister wives. We didn't have a lot, but we had each other."

"Should we go to Jeremiah's room?" Boone asks.

"I'm kind of scared," I tell him.

"It's okay. You don't have to."

"Can you look?" I ask him. "Just to make sure no one is there?"

He nods, and I turn to the kitchen as he steps into Jeremiah's bedroom. A moment later he joins me. "It's empty."

"Let's go to the church," I say.

Boone nods. "I agree."

We walk out the back door. I close it behind me out of habit, but there's nothing to keep in. Nothing that's going out. We walk around the property and I point out buildings. "That's where Bethany lives, and that's where the kids used to play. There's a fort back there in that tree line."

We enter the church, the metal doors scraping against the floor. "This is it," I fill in.

Boone nods, looking around. "I knew what to expect from the video that York got for Jeremiah's alibi, of him preaching here. But when I think of a church, I picture something more ornate. Not a concrete floor and folding chairs."

I walk to the front to the podium where Jeremiah would lead, giving his message several times a week. Most of his time was spent behind a locked door, where he spoke to God. And when he'd come to the front of the church, his four bishops beside him, he would lead us in prayer and in a service.

"Did you have music?" Boone asks.

"Yes," I say, "though none of the instruments are here. That's strange," I say, looking around. The keyboards are gone. The guitars, the microphones, and amps. "Okay, so the instruments are gone and the people and the vehicles, which means they left," I say.

"Where would they go?"

I twist my lip, a sinking feeling of doom. "Eden."

6

As we wend our way through the compound, a chill settles over me. I shove my hands into my winter coat, trying to stay warm.

"I forget how cold it is over the mountains," Boone says. "It's so much milder on the western side of the state."

I nod. "I'm surprised it's not snowing, actually."

"So, have you got any clues that could help us pin down the location of Eden?" Boone asks.

I shrug. "I know they were building bunkers somewhere. The women weren't allowed to know much more than that."

"How far away?" Boone asks.

"No idea. But the women were never

allowed there. The men were the ones who built it, who were working on it in case we needed shelter quickly, away from the government."

"Maybe that's where they are, then?"

"It's what Bethany said on the phone," I say as we walk over gravel and puddles of mud.

"Did you hear that?" Boone asks, frowning. Turning his head to the left.

I pause, listening, expecting to hear a barking dog or a squawking bird. Instead, I see a man. "It's Bishop Grove."

He's come out his door and is leaning against the doorframe, eyeing us, coughing.

I grab Boone's elbow. "Come on."

The fact that Boone carries a gun gives me a bit of relief, knowing that he will be able to protect us if necessary. I hope it doesn't come to that. But Bishop Grove has never been a man I care for. He and Bishop Isaiah were Jeremiah's right-hand men.

If forced to choose, I'd much rather see Grove. Our history isn't as entwined; my body has never been given to him. My body shakes at the memory as I struggle to repress it.

"What is it?" Boone asks.

"It's nothing," I say, my voice soft but the memories vivid, violent.

If Boone doubts the sincerity of my words, he doesn't press. I'm grateful. I am willing to share so many things with Boone—but that night? Never.

Jeremiah offering me as a gift to Isaiah, his closest friend, his brother in Christ. Though I was a grown woman in so many respects, I was still only sixteen, naïve to so much. Unable to use my voice to say no. I didn't even have access to that word—why would I refuse what my husband requested of me?

I didn't. I let Isaiah take me to his bed. I remember how my breasts ached, knowing Abel needed feeding, but I didn't want word to get back to my husband, the prophet, that I had refused to partake in the gift he wanted his closest confidant to have: me.

Jeremiah wanted me to feel special, raised up, coveted—that's how he spun it to me. But I felt none of those things. Not then, and certainly not now.

As we get closer, I notice the bishop's eyes are glassy, and he's leaning against his door-frame, his hand on his chest, as if in pain. I clear my throat. "Bishop Grove? Bishop Grove. It's me, Grace. Jeremiah's Grace."

I hate saying it like that, but I'm not quite sure how else to declare myself. I haven't been to the compound for a year, but I don't think he could forget me. After all, we'd been living in the same stretch of land for most of my life. He blessed the births of my children and lectured the congregation on respecting elders.

"Grace," he says slowly, "what are you doing here?"

"Are you all right?" I ask, now only a few yards from him. He coughs deeply, hacking into his elbow.

"I'm fine," he says, "I'm here doing the Lord's work. The prophet called on me."

"Called on you to do what?" I ask.

He shakes; his whole body seems to convulse. Part of me wonders if he's having a seizure, but before I can ask, his hands grip the doorframe.

"Where is everyone?" I ask.

"Why do you care?" He steps back, toward his door. "Didn't you leave?"

"It's true, I left," I tell him, "but my son, Abel, he's in trouble and—"

"They're not here," he says, narrowing his eyes at Boone.

"I know they're not here. We've been looking around. I went into my house and ..."

"You have no business being here," Bishop

Grove says. "You and whoever this man is should leave."

"We're looking for Abel," I tell him. "My son. I know he came back here and—"

"You're too late. They're gone," Grove repeats.

I gasp. Too late for what? I'm scared to know.

"Where did they go exactly?" Boone asks. "The bunkers?"

Grove frowns. "What do you know about them?"

Boone shrugs. "I know more than I should."

I'm scared of being here when everyone else is gone. I don't want to think about what being left behind implies.

I close my eyes, trying to think, trying to focus, but growing agitated at Grove's disregard for my need for more information. "Where did they go?" I repeat.

"They're on their retreat," Grove tells me. "It's that time of year."

"Retreat?" My mind spins, landing on the facts. "But the retreat is every other year," I say slowly. "And they went last year."

Boone asks me what I'm talking about.

I explain, "Jeremiah led a religious retreat

for all of his disciples. It was every other year and it was a big deal. All the families went."

"Where is it?" Boone asks.

"I'm not telling you where it is," Grove shouts. "I don't even know you." He looks pointedly at Boone before leaning down, bracing himself on his knees and coughing more deeply.

"Are you okay?" I ask him. "You seem—"

He shakes his head, but I see sweat on his forehead. And he wipes his brow, bracing himself again. Fear races through me. "Something's wrong," I say. "Do you need to sit down?"

He shakes his head. "No," he says. "Don't come closer to me."

"Did you take something? Did Jeremiah tell you to take something?" I ask him, "Something to take you home to Eden?"

Bishop Grove glares at me. "You wouldn't know anything about that, would you? You left the fold."

"I'm back," I say. "Tell me where they went. Did Jeremiah take everyone for the retreat at the same lodge as before?"

"I'm not telling you anything." He coughs loudly, then slams his hand to the door. "My oxygen," he says, walking into the house. "I need my oxygen, Grace."

Boone and I follow him inside, and I do as he asks. Grove sits down in an old recliner, and I pull over his oxygen machine.

It's then that I remember Bishop Grove was sick before he ever came to Garden Temple. He had lung cancer and came here while in remission. "Is this what you need?" I ask him. He nods, taking the tubes and shoving them into his nose, taking a big breath.

"You're okay," I say, realizing he hasn't been poisoned; he's just dying. "I really need to find my son," I tell him, not above begging.

"They're at the retreat," he tells me, looking away as if he is betraying someone by telling me this information.

"Where is it?" Boone asks.

"It's at Desert Mountain Lodge," I tell him.

The children loved it. It was the most luxurious time of the year. An opportunity for us to thank God for the blessings he bestowed upon us, according to Jeremiah. But I also know Jeremiah needed his people to remain happy, hopeful. And having a weekend at the lodge offered that.

"Enough," Grove says. "Let me sit here in peace. Go."

"Take care of yourself," Boone says to Bishop Grove before closing his front door.

"He's dying," I tell Boone as we walk to the car. "Cancer."

"Are you sure?" he asks.

I nod. "I remember him giving testimony about being sick before he joined the fold. He said he was in remission. God had cured him. It must have come back. Now it's taking his life."

"Why would they have left him here?" Boone asks. As a detective, it's his job to pick apart a story.

"I don't know," I say. "Maybe he wasn't well enough to go?"

"But doesn't he have a wife? Anyone who could have stayed?"

"He has several wives, so I don't know why he's alone," I say, remembering his wife, Martha, in particular. She was always so welcoming, and her household became a hub at the end of each summer, women filling her kitchen as we put up vegetables and fruit for winter.

"How far is it to this lodge?"

"Fifty minutes, an hour maybe."

"Do you know the way?" Boone asks, pulling out his phone.

I shake my head. "I couldn't get us there."

He searches the name of the lodge and calls their number. "It just keeps ringing and ringing," he says.

After a few minutes we give up. "It's forty miles away," he says. "Let's go."

7

As we drive away from the compound, an uncomfortable silence settles over the car. The space between Boone and I has grown somehow in the last hour. Inviting him into my old home, into the house I shared with Jeremiah, Lydia, Naomi and our children has given him access to parts of myself that shame me.

So I'm pulling back. I feel it as he drives away, the way my heart is getting tighter, fear rising higher in my chest, making it hard for me to breathe.

And it's not just Boone seeing my past—it's facing it head-on that scares me. It's the future. If something has happened to Abel, how will I survive? I unroll the window, taking in big gusts of air, desperate to push the fear aside as I breathe in deep.

"It's near freezing," he says, looking over at me as the wind whips my hair, as I hang out the window, looking down at the gravel that's as gray as my life here was. He must realize I need a moment because he doesn't say any more about the fact that he's trying to heat the car up at the same time as I'm cooling it down.

When my fingers are ice and my cheeks are raw, I roll up the window and lean back. Boone presses a button on the console, warming my seat. His thoughtfulness unnerves me. I look over at him, realizing how little I know about this man next to me.

I don't know where he grew up, what his parents are like. I know he has a sister, but does he care for her? How much? Would he fight for her? Would he give up everything for her? And his ex-wife, has he really moved past the life that they shared? Is he grieving the loss of his daughter every time I mention mine?

There are a million things I want to know of this man who is driving me toward my past. But asking them now seems impossible, like it will only create a wider divide between us. Pointing out our differences instead of finding the source of our common ground.

I'm scared all of his answers will be healthy, normal, typical. Sure, maybe he fought with his parents, or maybe he has a crazy uncle. Maybe he and his sister spent years hating one another. Maybe he and his ex-wife have hooked up since they signed their divorce papers. Honestly, I don't know, but I'm guessing that whatever mess he has in his past is a different kind of mess than mine.

And the mess I have is too dirty for a man as good as him to want to clean up.

"That was a lot back there. Right?" he says, looking straight ahead at the road.

I run my hands through my hair, my eyelids heavy, aching, tired. It's only four in the afternoon. I shouldn't be so sleepy, but I feel the weight of the day caving in on me. Grove's coughing fit is ringing in my ears.

"Why would Jeremiah leave him behind?" I ask.

"Who knows," he says. "Maybe Bishop Grove just wanted peace and quiet if he's ill. I'm sure everyone is at the lodge having some Bible study or something. Don't stress, Gray."

I smirk. *Bible study.* That's not what Jeremiah would be leading. He's not going to let people sit down and study the word of God.

He's the one who wants to be explaining it to them, deciphering the texts.

"I hope so," I tell him, not feeling very optimistic. Boone follows the GPS directions to the lodge. The drive is quiet besides the classical music that Boone turns on. After ten miles, I begin to appreciate why he likes it. It's steadying, soothing, comforting in a way I didn't expect. It sweeps me away as we drive and I let my eyes close for just a moment. When a sonata ends, I blink, looking around just in time.

"It's up there," I say, pointing to a sign on the side of the road for the Desert Mountain Lodge.

"You still tired?" he asks.

I shake my head, rubbing my eyes again. "No, I'm fine. I just need to find Abel and Bethany."

"I know," he says softly.

When we get to the lodge, I immediately begin scanning the parking lot.

"You recognize any of these vehicles?" Boone asks.

I shake my head. "I don't know. They all look the same, you know?"

We get out of his car and he locks the doors. I have my purse on my shoulder and Boone at my side. In a different life, maybe we would be walking to this lodge together, hand in hand, for a getaway, a night away from the kids. I suppress my disappointment in what life gave me. Knowing that fantasy is so far from my reality, it's not even funny.

"What?" Boone asks, noticing my expression change.

"I was just thinking about how weird this is, to be here with you."

"At the lodge or on this road trip?"

"Both. All of it. I hardly know you."

Boone's eyebrow lifts. "I find that a bit offensive," he says.

"Really?"

"Yeah," he says. "I don't open up to many people."

"And what, the way you've been with me, that's opening up?" I lift my eyes, irritated with Boone's inability to see how unusual this situation is for me. How intense it all feels. How hard it is to be away from my girls. How far Abel feels from me.

He scoffs, not liking where this is going. "Can we not argue?" he says. "I don't want to fight, not after the day we've had, the week you've had. God, Gray, you haven't had a break."

"I won't ever get a break," I say tightly, thinking of the life sprawled out ahead of me. How many fires am I going to have to put out raising three children on my own?

I hope it's three children. I hope Abel's here.

"Hey," Boone says, "I keep losing you. Ever since you were at the compound, you've been ..."

"What," I say. "Distant?"

"Yeah," he says, "lost."

"Makes sense. Because I do feel lost right now, uncertain and scared. My kids are my whole world," I tell him, "and if we don't find Abel ..." My voice cracks. We stop on the sidewalk leading to the lodge, the air cold and my heart so damn heavy. I'm tired of being the only one to hold it.

"I know," he says as he opens the door of the lodge, holding it for me. "But we are going to find him just like we found Ruthie. *You* found Ruthie. It's going to be okay." He smiles, and I appreciate his attempt at making things better, even if only a fraction. It's sure a hell of a lot nicer to be around a man like this than to be around a man whose intent is to make things worse.

I walk to the front desk. The lodge looks

like it's been dropped out of a hunting catalog. Plaid everywhere, antlers on the doors, taxidermy on the mantel. The woman at the desk smiles.

"Hi, I'm Samantha. Do you have a reservation?"

"No," I say, "I'm looking for someone. Jeremiah Priest. Is he a guest here?"

She frowns. "I'm not sure I can actually tell you that," she says, laughing nervously.

"He's my husband."

She looks at Boone behind me.

"I'm a police officer." Boone flashes his badge, and the woman's eyes widen.

"Oh, I didn't realize."

I nod. "Yes, it's an emergency."

"I see. Okay, just a sec. Priest?" she says.

"Yes. P-R-I-E-S-T."

"All right." Her fingers *click-clack* on the keyboard, then she frowns. "I'm sorry. There's no Jeremiah Priest here."

"What about Abel Priest? Lydia Priest? Naomi Priest?" I say, my voice getting higher, tighter, scared.

She starts typing more fervently. "I'm sorry. I don't know."

Boone steps forward. "I know this is not a normal circumstance. Is there any chance that you are having a large gathering here right now? We're looking for a group of about two hundred people. Jeremiah Priest is the one who's leading the retreat."

She bites her bottom lip, thinking. "No, but Jeremiah *does* have retreats here sometimes." She smiles, realizing who we're talking about. "Okay, sorry. I was just a little flustered. Yeah, there's no booking for them. They were here last winter though. I think it was the last week of February? Maybe the first week of March."

I nod, thinking that sounds about right. "So you're sure they're not here now?"

"Nope, not here." Samantha frowns. "Would you like a coupon? Ten percent off your stay!"

Boone takes it from her. "Thanks."

"Of course. If you have any other questions, just call."

"Right," I say. "Will do."

We walk out of the lodge and get in Boone's car. My shoulders slump as I buckle myself in. "Dammit!" I say. I don't usually swear, but the word falls out. "If they're not here, where are they, Boone?"

He runs his hand over his eyebrows. "I don't know," he says, "but we'll find out.

"Grove was lying to me," I say. "He just lied right to my face."

"You sure he's dying of cancer?"

I shrug. "I mean, I assumed so. He was on the oxygen tank."

"His eyes though. He seemed all bent out of shape, didn't he?" Boone presses.

I nod. "At first, yes, that's what I assumed. But then he said he needed his oxygen and wanted to sit down."

"At first, did you think he'd been poisoned?" Boone asks me as he starts the engine.

"That's exactly what I thought."

"Well, maybe he was or maybe he wasn't. However, he told us Jeremiah was at a retreat. You were the one who said it was this lodge."

I exhale, realizing Boone is right. I filled in the gaps and I made an error. "What are we going to do?" I ask.

Boone reverses his car, pulling out of the parking lot. "We're going to go find the Grant County sheriff and report two hundred missing people."

8

THE SHERIFF'S office in Grant County is a lot different than the police station in Downtown Tacoma, where Boone works. We pull up to a big brick building, with landscaping that is on its last legs, dirt and concrete, rocks doubling as sculptures.

"I'm going to let you do the talking," I tell Boone as he pulls open the door for me once more, this time not entering a rustic lodge, instead entering a place where I'm guessing he will be very comfortable.

"I'm on it," he says. "I want answers just as badly as you do."

It's after six o'clock by now, and the young woman at the desk looks like she's ready to leave, heavy eyes looking down at her phone, even though I know this place is open twenty-four hours a day. "I'm looking for a senior detective," Boone tells her.

"Sheriff Martindale?" she asks, tucking her wavy blonde hair behind her ears. "I'm not sure if he's in; give me a sec." She picks up her phone. Before tapping any numbers, she smiles at Boone. "Who's asking for him?"

"My name's Orion Boone," he says, flashing her his badge. "I'm a detective in Tacoma, Washington. This is official business."

"Is he expecting you?" she asks, narrowing her eyes.

"No," Boone says, "but it's urgent."

"Of course," she says. "One moment." She sets the phone down and stands from her desk, walking around a corner. She calls out, "Drew, someone's here for you from Tacoma, one of those officers that was here last week about that little girl."

A moment later, Drew Martindale walks into the foyer offering Boone his hand. "Hello, Detective, how can I help you?"

Boone shows him his badge and then tucks it back into his jacket. "This isn't about the missing child," he says, "but it *is* about her father."

"Jeremiah Priest?" Martindale asks. He's an

older man with a big potbelly, his shirt tucked into his pants and his belt buckle a giant star, as if he belongs in Texas, a lone ranger.

I press my lips together, clasping my hands, refusing to say anything that might jeopardize Boone's questioning. We need Martindale on our side. I need his help, and I'm not going to put my foot in my mouth and ruin anything. I know if I start blabbering about sister wives and the second coming, I'll sound like a crazy person.

"Can we have a word with you?" Boone says.

"Sure, of course, right this way. Tammi, can you get us some coffee?"

I smile at the thought of coffee as he leads us into his office. Boone and I both take a seat opposite him. He sits behind a big oak desk. He has a framed photo of a nice-looking family dressed in red and green, on a bookshelf, a boy and a girl, both teenagers. And I wonder how he would feel if something happened to them. If he lost them. I can appeal to this part of him and hope it helps our cause.

I want him to be sympathetic to my situation. I want him to see things from my point of view, how urgent this is, how dire.

"So what's this about, if it's not about the

girl?" Martindale asks, leaning back in his chair. He has a gray mustache and thinning hair, gold wire-rimmed glasses across the bridge of his nose.

"Jeremiah Priest is missing," Boone says, "along with everyone he lives with at the compound. We came here looking for Gray West's son, Abel, a child she had with Mr. Priest, and neither of them are at home. In fact, no one is at home. No one is at the entire compound."

Martindale frowns as Tammi brings in the coffee along with a can of powdered creamer. "Thanks, sweetheart." Martindale gives her a wink that is less fatherly and more lewd. It makes my skin crawl.

I take my coffee black, indulging in a long gulp. It tastes disgusting.

"Look, I don't know what you want me to do here, Boone. That mother, the one with the missing child?" I don't clear my throat and tell him I am that mother. "She caused a whole bunch of problems here for no good reason. Jeremiah may be a little religious, but he's harmless. He's lived out on that property for twenty years, maybe more. He's never hurt anybody. He pays his taxes, and he hasn't even sent his kids to public school. He homeschools the whole lot. One of his crews put a new roof on my sister's house last summer; they did a great job. Gave 'er a ten percent discount for no good reason except the kindness of his heart. That is the kind of man you want in your community."

"You're saying you want a man like Jeremiah Priest in your community?" Boone asks. His voice is steady.

"Look, the mother of that missing girl, she had a whole bunch of police officers crowding this room a few days ago, insistent that Jeremiah was a kidnapper, but was he? No. It turns out that woman's kid was a few doors down at her neighbor's house that whole time. I don't know about you, but I feel like she's a conspiracy theorist." He looks over at me, and I realize he knows exactly who I am. He smirks, playing dumb, but when he chuckles at my indignation, I can't sit by.

"I am not a conspiracy theorist. I lived there with Jeremiah for fifteen years."

Martindale smiles widely as if I'm proving his point.

"We need help. I'm just a mother looking for my son."

"Last week it was your daughter, now it's your son?" Martindale asks wryly. "Oh, honey, give it a rest. You want that man back? Well, maybe you should put on a little makeup and try harder."

Boone raises a hand. "Excuse me. That is completely uncalled for."

"Hey, we're not big-city folk like you got over there in Tacoma. We're good people, salt of the earth. We believe in God and make our promises on the Bible. Don't we, Tammi?" he calls out. Tammi lifts her hand, giving a thumbs-up, having no idea what she's agreeing to.

"I'm not coming after my ex-husband. I'm looking for my son, that's all."

Martindale smiles. "The thing is, you say they're missing, but they're not."

"How can you be so certain?" I ask.

"When Jeremiah was here, he made it clear to me that in a few days' time he was taking his entire congregation, the church that meets at that property of his, on a religious retreat. Look, that's his right as an American; he can go pray wherever he likes. However he likes."

"Well, where was he going?" I ask. "Because one of the guys who lives on the property said that they were going on a retreat. I thought it might be to the Desert Mountain Lodge, but we were just there and Jeremiah wasn't."

"It's not my job to keep tabs on him," Martindale says, then lifts his hands, looking at Boone as if he might agree with him. "You need to settle this woman down. People might get the wrong idea."

"And what idea might that be?" Boone asks.

Martindale chuckles. "Look, all I'm saying is maybe her husband left her for a reason."

I seethe at this, my fingernails digging into my palms, and I swear I'll draw blood. I want to scream. I want to shout. I want to yell at this man who is so condescending. So patronizing. How did he become an elected official anyway? The sheriff of Grant County?

Boone, though, knowing how upset I am, places a hand on my forearm. "Hey, so I think we're all done here."

"Done here?" I ask. "We haven't *done* anything." I look at Martindale. "You have to help me. I'm desperate."

Martindale smiles. "Oh, I can see that, honey."

"Don't call me honey."

Martindale stands. "Okay, sweetheart. Well, the fact is Jeremiah was here a few days ago. He told me he was going along with his whole compound on a little road trip. They're going to go pray to the high heavens. I don't know. It's none of my business, and it doesn't seem like it's yours. If he left you, he left you; you have no more business with him."

"But he has my son."

"And how old is this missing son of yours?"

"He'll be sixteen next week," I say.

Martindale grins. "Seems like he's old enough to know what he wants to do, and maybe he doesn't want to be with you."

My jaw drops at this man's grotesque abuse of power. "How dare you?" I ask. "This is going to blow up in your face. People are going to die."

I don't know if that is true, but I want this man to see the gravity of the situation. And to me, it feels like life or death.

Boone takes my arm, leading me out of the office. "We're leaving." His voice is firm and direct. There's no thank-you. No I appreciate your time, thanks for the help—nothing. Boone is not going to coddle this man, who is so clearly inferior.

"Keep walking," Boone tells me as we pass Tammi's desk and head straight out the front doors. It's dark now; the sky is black, and I'm hungry and tired, and the coffee certainly didn't do its job.

"Damn it," I say. "Damn it, Boone." I drop

down to the ground, sitting on my heels. It's not supposed to be this difficult to just live a nice, happy life.

Boone, though, is not letting me fall apart, not here, not at the station. He grabs my hand and pulls me up. "Get in the car," he says. "We're not giving them the satisfaction of watching you have a meltdown."

"This isn't a meltdown," I cry. "This is a mother's heart breaking. We're running out of time, Boone."

"Don't let it break." Boone's words are soft, but his voice is harsh.

"Are you mad at me?" I wipe my eyes, trying to get a grip on myself.

"You should have let me handle that, Gray. You put your emotions first, and that's not going to help us. We need to be smart. You can cry later."

His words are a jolt of reality, and I need them, even if they are hard to hear.

"You've got to stay strong," Boone says, yanking open my door, slamming it shut behind me. I jump at the noise, and then he pulls out of the parking lot.

We drive for a mile, turn into a diner. "Come on," he says. "You need to eat; you're a mess. And you need some coffee. I didn't realize how often you needed that fuel."

I wipe my eyes, wanting to yell at him, wanting to do something to prove my point—that Martindale is awful—but Boone already knows. I would be preaching to the choir.

"Come on, Gray," he repeats. "I mean it, you need to eat some food, and we need to make a plan."

"A plan?" I ask. "But we don't know where to look."

Boone smiles. "You brought a detective with you for a reason, right? We'll get to the bottom of this, Gray. I'm not giving up on you. So you sure as hell can't give up on me."

9

THE DINER IS NEARLY EMPTY, which is surprising since it's dinnertime. But then maybe not, considering we're in the middle of nowhere on the side of a highway. If it were summer, there'd be tumbleweeds outside this window. Instead, it's just rolling dirt hills and a long black highway stretching forever.

A waitress hands us plastic menus while she smacks her gum, tapping her pen to a pad of paper. "I'm Jana. Just give me a holler when you're ready to order. The meatloaf's on special tonight, but it isn't any good. Don't let the cook hear me tell you that." She gives us a smile, her frosty-blue eye shadow brightening her face. And I appreciate her down-to-earth warmth, a sharp contrast to Martindale. Exactly what I need.

"What sounds good?" Boone asks, flipping the menu over.

"Not the meatloaf," I say.

He smiles. "When I'm at a diner, I usually order bacon and eggs, some French toast." He smiles. I don't.

I don't feel like smiling. I feel like taking a really hot shower and crying myself to sleep. I knew this would be hard, but it feels impossible.

"Come on, Gray. I can smile. You can smile too. I don't think I could do my job if every time I got to a dead end, I fell apart."

I frown. "I'm not falling apart," I say, but I know that's not true. And I know I'm being a brat. Boone is being nothing but kind to me, and I need to pull up my bootstraps and toughen up.

Sighing, I answer his original question. "I'm not a breakfast-for-dinner kind of person."

"No?" Boone says. "I wouldn't have guessed it."

I smirk, wondering why he's so nice to me as he waves Jana over. "You'd better know what you're getting because I'm hungry," he says.

"That food we ate from the gas station at noon did not tide me over."

"I didn't realize you had such an appetite."

"I do," he says. "I'm a grown man."

I laugh. "Oh my gosh, what am I going to do with you?"

Boone smiles. "I sure as hell hope we find out."

The waitress asks what we'd like. After Boone orders, I tell her, "I'll take the grilled cheese and tomato soup, and some coffee with cream."

"Coming right up," she says. She walks away with our menus in hand and comes back a moment later pouring the coffee that's probably burnt but will taste better than what they were serving at the station.

I reach for a container of half-and-half, pulling back the paper tab, pouring it into my coffee, stirring it with the metal spoon longer than I need to. Letting it swallow up the silence.

"Did you want to talk about today?" Boone asks as I take a sip of coffee.

I groan. "Where do we even start?"

"I take it you don't like long car rides?"

I laugh sharply. "That was not the problem with the day."

"I know. I was just wondering."

"Actually, I don't like long car rides. I hate them. I don't like driving at all. I would give up my keys forever if I could."

"Really? If you won the lottery, you'd get a full-time chauffeur?"

"Exactly," I say. "I'd be like someone in a movie with a Town Car waiting outside my front door every time I wanted to go to the grocery store."

Boone chuckles. "That's funny."

"I wasn't joking," I say, but I crack a smile. "What about you?" I ask. "Do you like long car rides?"

He lifts his shoulders, then lets them fall. "I don't know about *like*, but I don't hate them. I spend a lot of the time in the car on my job waiting, watching."

"Is it hard?" I ask him. "Your job?"

He nods. "It's harder ever since I lost Suzanne. I've always worked around the deceased, but I could separate my emotions. Then I lost my little girl, and suddenly it all became more real, more personal, and it made the job a lot more difficult."

"Had you ever lost anyone before you lost her?" I ask him.

"No, not really. No one I loved."

"I'm sorry."

"I know you are," he says, and he takes a drink of his coffee as the waitress brings our food.

"So what are we going to do?" I ask the detective.

He pours syrup over his French toast and takes a bite. "I think we'll have to go back to the compound, right? Clearly we missed something."

"That was what I was thinking. Tonight?"

"No," Boone says. "We're not going back there tonight. We're going to go back in broad daylight."

"Does the place creep you out?" I ask.

He nods. "I felt like I was walking around on some true crime show when I was out there. Besides, we won't find any clues in the dark."

"I always used to wonder what my parents would think if they saw where I ended up living. When I was little, I loved going to school. I loved the science fair projects, and back-to-school night, and parent-teacher conferences. I was a really annoying little kid, who always insisted on knowing everything my teachers had to say about me. When I moved to Garden Temple with my aunt and uncle, I knew my parents would have been so sad to see what happened to their bright, straight-A student."

I sink into the memory, a sad smile on my face. "Life is so weird, you know. When I was little, I was so sure my life would go one way, but it's gone the exact opposite. And I look back now, and I think maybe I could have stopped it, you know, before Jeremiah took me as his wife. Maybe I could have run away or asked for help, but where? You saw how far out the compound is. I don't think I would've gotten very far if I had tried to run. Someone would have stopped me."

"We can't live our lives with regret," Boone says. "It will stop you from ever finding happiness."

"I think you're right," I say. "Even though it took longer than I would have liked, when I finally got the strength to leave Garden Temple, I never once regretted it. My parents would have been proud of me."

"How did you end up in Tacoma?"

"Ideally, we would have gone to Wenatchee. My mom inherited this old family farm out there. Since they were teachers, we would have summers off and spring break and Christmas vacation, and we'd go up to the farm, swing in the big old trees, swim in the lake, pick apples in the fall."

"Why didn't you go there?"

"My uncle sold the property to pay off my parents' debts. But a small farm wouldn't have worked anyway. I needed to disappear in a big city far from the compound. Tacoma was less expensive than Seattle."

"You thought it out," Boone says. "But where did you get money?"

"I stole a little every month for a year, from our grocery budget. It only added up to enough for gas and a few months at the motel. It was a hard time once we got to Tacoma."

"You got through though," Boone says. "I bet your parents would have been pretty proud of that."

We finish our food. Our game plan is pretty shaky, but at least tomorrow we'll go to the compound and try to find clues. Maybe Bishop Grove will tell us something else.

After we eat and Boone pays the bill, we drive to a motel that we saw on our way to the restaurant. We get out of the car with our suitcases, ready to check into our rooms. I pause.

"What?" Boone asks.

"I know it's totally not appropriate, and I

know you're a detective, and I'm..." I shake my head.

"I'm not a detective right now. Martindale sure as hell doesn't want law enforcement involved, so I'm operating as a rogue officer. So, what is this inappropriate thing you wanted to mention?"

"I don't want to sleep in a room by myself tonight," I tell him. "I'm scared to be alone right now."

Boone nods and takes my bag. "Come on, Gray. Let's go get ourselves a motel room."

Later when we're checked into the two-star motel, with the door locked, after I've showered, I lie down on one of the queen-sized beds. My hair is damp against the pillowcase. The shower is running as Boone cleans up.

I pull out my phone to call Luna. The girls answer, all smiles, with big, bright stories of their day. I try not to cry. I want them to know that I'm safe. That they're safe. That Abel will be safe soon.

"Are you coming home tomorrow?" Ruthie asks. "With Abel and Bethany?"

"Soon," I tell her. "Real soon. I'm just tired, and so we're going to bed now, but tomorrow we're going to go get him, okay?"

"Okay, Mommy, I love you so much," Ruthie says.

She gets off the phone, and I ask Olive how she's really doing. "Does Ruthie seem okay?" I ask her.

"Yes. Honestly, Mom, Ruthie seems like herself. I know it was scary being kidnapped and all, but she's happy. Luna kept us really busy all day and basically let us do whatever we wanted, so..."

I laugh softly. "Good. I want you to be happy."

"I want you to be happy too, Mom."

"I don't want you to stay up too late, okay?"

"I won't," Olive says. "I know how to take care of myself. You were practically married at my age."

"Don't say that," I say, "please."

"Sorry," she says, "bad joke."

"Yeah, really bad joke. But call me if you need anything, all right?"

"Of course. I love you, Mom."

"I love you too."

Olive hands the phone to Luna, and I thank her again for everything.

"Don't mention it," she says. "Just go get your son, and come home safe."

"I'm trying," I tell her.

"Oh," Luna adds, "so are you sharing a room with the hot detective?"

I roll my eyes. "Something like that."

Luna groans. "Just so you know, I'm living vicariously through you. Not the terrible parts, just the sexy ones."

"This is not sexy."

"Whatever you say, Gray." Luna laughs as we're hanging up.

Boone comes out of the bathroom, drying his hair with a towel, wearing sweats and a white T-shirt. "What's not sexy?" he asks.

I chuckle. "Please, don't."

He laughs. "I'm not doing anything. So we've already covered the fact that you don't like road trips, but how do you feel about late-night television?"

"It's not that late," I say. "It's like, what, eight o'clock?"

Boone grins. "Reality TV or drama?"

"I don't usually watch TV," I admit.

"Okay, so that means *The Great British Baking Show* will be a real treat, right?"

I smile, very much appreciating the idea of watching people with lovely accents bake cakes. He turns it on, surprising me once again.

"I'm rooting for the young kid," he tells me. "He made one nice-looking soufflé."

"You really watch this?" I ask, looking over at him.

He's in his bed, the remote in his hand, turning up the volume. "Yeah, but don't talk. I don't want to miss the opening."

10

WE WAKE EARLY. It's just after six o'clock and we're both ready for the day, dressed and at the diner again. This time I do order breakfast, and Boone gets the same as me, hash browns and eggs.

"Okay, so let's go over the game plan," Boone says.

"Good thinking." I begin rehashing what we talked about last night after Boone's favorite contestant won Star Baker. "We're going to drive to the compound. Once we're there, we're going to talk to Bishop Grove, hopefully. If he isn't willing, we'll just start looking through Jeremiah's bedroom and his office at the church. Surely we'll find something in one of those places, and then we'll start going after leads."

Boone smiles, pouring Tabasco on his potatoes. "See, I really do think you could be a detective. You ever think about going to the academy?"

I laugh. "Boone, I don't even have a high school diploma."

Fork in hand, he points it at me. "You know, I'm glad you brought that up. We're going to have to do something about that when things settle down."

I eat my pancake. "When things settle down? I don't know if that is what my life will ever be. Settled."

"Maybe you're right," he teases. "I mean, worst-case scenario, you're a hot mess forever, and you need to keep me around to help you stay in one piece."

I lift an eyebrow. "For the record, I do not need a man to keep me in one piece."

He takes a drink of his coffee. "I know, I know. I'm not going to go all male chauvinist on you like Drew Martindale."

"God, he was such a disappointment," I say as we finish up our food.

Back in the car, we listen to talk radio, and I

learn that Boone has a penchant for listening to the news in the morning on his drive in to work.

"I see, so you're not always listening to classical music."

"No," he says. "I'm very well rounded."

"Right," I say, thinking this mountain of a man is not exaggerating. He is, in a word, perfect, which makes all my own insecurities seem even larger than life.

When we arrive, the compound echoes with the same sense of eeriness we felt yesterday as if there are ghosts walking around this place, haunting me with memories of my past.

"Should we go talk to Bishop Grove first?" I ask.

Boone nods. We park the car in front of my old house and walk over to the one where we spoke to Bishop Grove just yesterday. It feels so much longer ago than that. We knock on the door and I see a light inside. I call out for him, but no one answers. "That's strange," I say. "Yesterday, he was really willing to talk to us."

"I wonder what's changed," Boone says as I knock more loudly, calling out for Bishop Grove more aggressively.

"On a scale of one to ten, how inappropriate would it be for us to just push open the door?" I ask Boone.

"I feel like we're past scales right now, and appropriate was thrown out the window a few days ago."

Boone's right. There's an urgency to the situation now that is unfathomable. "You have your gun?" I ask.

Boone nods. "You think I'll need it?"

"I don't know what to think," I say as I wrap my fingers around Bishop Grove's doorknob, opening it.

Inside, it's dead silent. I call out for the bishop, hoping to hear something, but there's nothing. In the living room, his oxygen tank is beside an empty recliner. There's a glass of water but not much else. A Bible, a half-eaten sandwich.

I frown. "Maybe he's upstairs."

Boone nods, taking in the room, then leads the way up the stairs with his gun drawn, me following as we pass the bedrooms. I've been in here before plenty of times. The bishop's wife, Martha, was really good at canning, and every fall we'd wind up in her kitchen with mason jars and cucumbers and apples, whatever bumper crop we had—peaches and plums and pears—stocking our shelves for the winter ahead. God's work, we called it. We were so proud of the full pantry shelves.

My time in Martha's kitchen was happy. I liked being with the women, our aprons on, our hair frizzy, sweat running down our necks. The windows wide open, and the kids running in and out of the yard into the house, happy. A big stainless-steel pot on the stove, sanitizing the jars to be filled. Apple pie filling mixed by one of the wives, another making a pickle brine.

I wonder if I will ever have happy moments like that with my neighbors on my street in Tacoma. Luna and Kendall and Julia, all very different kinds of housewives, wearing their fancy leggings and pushing their jogging strollers, holding to-go cups of coffee with manicured fingers. Different, but maybe not in any of the ways that matter. They're good, kind women with big hearts. Women who love taking care of their children. Just the same as the women who gathered here at Garden Temple did. We just accessorize our lives differently.

Sometimes I wonder if the divide is as great

as I once thought. Maybe deep down women are all more alike than we are different. I find solace in that thought, even now, as I climb these steps to the second story of Bishop Grove's house, looking for a man who I don't care for at all.

I call out his name, hoping to find him.

"He's in here," Boone says, standing in a door that is wide open. The man on the bed is stick still, gray. Gone.

"He's dead," I say, stepping closer, gagging at the smell. I don't know what took his life, but I can make a few guesses. It wasn't cancer. Not last night.

"Do you think it was poison?" Boone asks.

I nod. Looking at the glass on his bedside table, peering into it, not daring to touch it. I point to the chalky residue at the bottom of the glass. "It must have been. I hope we aren't too late, Boone."

There is a clear plastic baggie that is empty. Beside it, a note on a small slip of paper written in my husband's hand:

BISHOP GROVE,

When it is time, be strong. Eden is waiting. You will be rewarded.

Forever in eternity,
Your Prophet Jeremiah Priest

"But why would he have stayed behind?" Boone asks.

My throat tightens. "Maybe to warn us off in case we showed up. I don't know."

"You think Jeremiah would have kept him here in case you came?"

"I don't know what Jeremiah would do," I say, looking at Bishop Grove. His face blank, his eyes staring up at the ceiling. He may have been here like this for twenty-four hours.

"I don't want to stay in this room another moment. Come on," I say.

"I'm not calling this in," Boone says. "I know I'm supposed to, but if we do that, it's gonna tie us up at the damn sheriff's office, and we'll never find your boy."

We leave Bishop Grove's house the same way we came in, shutting the door. We spend hours searching the compound for clues. In the church we look through drawers, through closets. In houses we search the rooms of the bishop's. "Maybe Micah's house has something that could be a lead," I suggest, and we trudge over to the home of the man who took so much from me. A man as evil, in my eyes, as Jeremiah is.

"This house creeps me out," Boone says, and he has no idea how deeply I feel the same thing.

The compound feels empty, and after hours of looking, we finally face the home where I raised my children, our feet crunching over the cold gravel, our breath frosty in the air.

Inside this house for a second time, hoping an additional search will reveal more, I flip on the lights. "Come on," I say. "Let's go to Jeremiah's bedroom. We might find something there."

Boone nods, agreeing with me, and I lead the way. Yesterday, I was too disgusted to step inside Jeremiah's bedroom. But now I do it without recoiling. Now I just need answers.

"As wives," I explain to Boone as we step inside, "we never slept with him here. He would come to us. He wanted to keep one space to himself, one private place of his own."

Boone nods, not pressing me for details, and I know why. This is uncomfortable, to say the least, discussing my sex life with him. I don't want to discuss it with anyone, ever. There are too many terrible moments I shared with Jeremiah.

But at least they weren't in this room because right now I need to look at this space with open eyes, a clear head, not thinking of Bishop Grove's dead body, thinking instead of my son's life, praying that he's still living, that there wasn't some pact for everyone to take the pills Bishop Grove did and take their lives last night.

"Do you see anything in here?" I ask as we begin rooting through dresser drawers, looking under the bed.

"There's a safe," Boone says. He's opened the closet doors, and inside there's a black box. "Do you think you can crack the code?"

I run my fingers around the dial, wondering what the combination might be. I try Jeremiah's birthday. It doesn't work.

"What date mattered to him?" Boone asks.

I press my lips together, and I enter my anniversary: 06132006. It opens. Of course it does. It feels like everything with Jeremiah comes back to me.

"What was that combination?" Boone asks.

"The day I married him."

When it clicks open, I exhale, not even realizing I'd been holding my breath. Boone crouches down alongside me, and together we peer into the safe. It's full of paperwork and books, a Bible. We pull everything out and sit on Jeremiah's bed. I hate that I'm sitting on this mattress, that my body presses against his sheets, a quilt I sewed. It feels wrong. Dirty. I feel sick just thumbing through his paperwork, knowing he touched it, thinking of how he touched me. My body starts to shake, tears form in my eyes, and I hate how weak I feel.

Boone stops searching and moves closer to me.

"Hey," Boone says, "we don't have to do this right now. We can go back to the motel, get some food at the diner, do this later. It's already getting dark out."

"No," I say, thinking of my son. Of Bethany. Of the children my sister wives brought into the world. So much innocence that Jeremiah is taking. "Boone, we don't have time."

"You need to let me know when it gets to be too much," he says.

We start looking through the papers. It's a bunch of deeds to properties. "Maybe he didn't sell them all," Boone says.

"I guess not," I say. "Maybe he held on to things for when he might need money later."

"What's this?" Boone asks, holding up a piece of paper. It's a list of names. "Do you recognize them?" On the top of the piece of paper, Jeremiah has written, *Exiled Members of Garden Temple*. There are many names I don't know, along with a date beside each one, marking the day on which they left the fold. Dating back to the beginning.

I scan down the list. Many of these people would have left the congregation when I was still a teenager. But as my finger slides down the list, over fifty names in all, I stop near the bottom. "Her," I say, "Genevieve Wilder."

"You know her?" Boone asks.

I nod in disbelief. "Kind of. I remember her, at least. We were about the same age. She came here after Ruthie was born. But the thing is," I say, turning toward Boone, "I didn't think she left."

"What did you think happened?"

"Jeremiah told us that she died."

"Died?" he asks. "How?"

"He told us she died in a car crash, that she'd gone to visit her family, which she probably shouldn't have been doing. He said she died in a head-on collision. I remember all of us crying, hating the idea of her life being lost, but maybe that's not what happened at all. If she left of her own accord..."

"What?" Boone asks. "What are you thinking?"

"If she is alive, she might have some information. I'm thinking she might've left for a reason, and we need to know what that reason was."

11

WE LEAVE the compound and get into Boone's car, cranking up the heat. I'm shaken from seeing Bishop Grove in his bed, gray and cold, and walking through the home where I spent so many years living has brought my past to my present in a way that I never wanted to see happen. Boone is patient and quiet, holding the stack of papers that we took from Jeremiah's study.

"Nothing here can be of too much value," he says, "unless he was planning on returning."

"Well, he isn't going to ever come back," I say. "This is his endgame. This is it now; it's happening."

Boone nods. "Maybe we can get a contact for Genevieve from Charlie."

With my agreement, we quickly make the call, and Charlie sounds relieved to hear us.

"I've been worried sick," she says. "Do you have an update? Did you find your son?"

"No," I say. But I fill her in on the exiled members list.

"So what now?" she asks.

"We have a name for a woman named Genevieve who left Garden Temple," I tell her, explaining how I thought Genevieve was killed in a car crash. I'm wondering now if maybe that was simply a story Jeremiah told us to protect himself.

"Let me pull up the database," Charlie says.

I almost tell her about Bishop Grove, but Boone catches on and shakes his head, cutting me off. I hold back. Right now Boone is not on duty, but Charlie is. There's a difference, even if it's miniscule.

"It looks like she has her last address in Ritzville. That's just over an hour from where you are now," Charlie says.

"Can you text that to me?" Boone asks.

"Of course, but you guys sound tired. You need to get some sleep. It's late already, and you've been driving a lot."

"I know," I say, "but if we stop now, we might be too late. We might miss something."

"I know you're worried," she says, "but you have a long day ahead of you tomorrow. Make sure you take care of yourselves tonight, okay?"

"Thanks, Charlie," I say before we end the call. She texts Boone Genevieve's address as well as her last known phone number.

I immediately punch in the number that Charlie texted us for Genevieve. Her phone rings and rings and rings. When voice mail picks up, I clear my throat. "Hi, Genevieve. You might not remember me. My name's Grace. I used to live with you at Garden Temple. I'm sure you're trying to block that time out of your memory—so am I. Please give me a call back at this number. It would mean a lot. An awful lot." I end the call and groan. "Well, that's a dead end."

"No," Boone says, "it's not. It's a hiccup. It's a sign that we need to go get some food and some rest and pick up again tomorrow.

"I wanted her to answer. I want to drive out to Ritzville and talk to her right now."

"She's not going to know where Abel is," Boone tells me plainly. "If she left the fold years ago, she's not going to have any information on where they could be right now."

"That's not what I want to hear," I say.

"I know it's not," Boone says, "but it's the

truth. Seeing her might help stir up a memory, and that is important, but we're not driving out to Ritzville right now. It's late. It's after seven, and she's not picking up her phone. We've been up since the crack of dawn, hardly got any sleep yesterday. It's not responsible."

I press my lips together, knowing he's right, but not wanting to say so. He pulls his car out of the gravel road and heads back to the main highway toward the diner and the motel where we stayed last night. The drive is silent. We've spent the whole day talking, and there's nothing left to say. Knowing we are pausing our mission to find Abel makes me ill.

"Do you want to eat inside?" Boone asks as we pull up to the diner.

"Not really hungry," I say, sick to my stomach.

"Wait here," he says. "I'll get us some food to go."

He heads into the diner, and I use the time to pull out my phone and call Luna to see if I can talk to my girls. Luna puts Olive on the phone right away.

"Hey, Mom," she says. "I miss you."

She sounded a lot more chipper yesterday, and I'm wondering if the weight of the last week is finally catching up to her too. It's heavy in a way I wish she didn't have to experience.

"How was school?" I ask. "Is Ruthie all right?"

"Ruthie's okay," she says. "She's right here. Say hi, Ruthie."

"Hi, Mama." Ruthie's voice lights up my heart.

"Oh, just a sec," Olive says.

A moment later, the phone call connects to FaceTime, and just like that, I see my little girls.

"We should have done this last night," I say. "I always forget about this feature." I'm still getting used to the modern technology that I went so many years without.

"You look tired," Olive says. "Where are you?"

"I'm in Boone's car. He went to get us some dinner, but I am tired," I tell them honestly.

"Did you find Abel?" Ruthie asks. "Did you talk to Bethany? Are they coming home?"

"I didn't find them yet," I say. "They weren't home when I got there."

"Does Lydia know where they are, or Naomi?" Olive asks, confused.

"You know, it doesn't sound like they know either," I say, protecting them, not wanting to tell them that the two hundred people they grew up with have vanished in plain sight. I don't want to confuse their hearts any more than they already are.

"Do you think you'll be home tomorrow?" Olive asks.

"I hope so," I say, "but it might be another night. Are you okay there with Luna?"

"Yeah," Olive says, and I know she's putting on a brave face. "They're really nice here, and Sophie's been awesome. One of her friends that she's in drama club with came over today, and they painted our faces."

Ruthie smiles. "They made me a cat," she says. "Next year for Halloween, I'm going to be a kitten; is that okay?"

"Sure, baby. That sounds great," I say. "Well, I'm glad you're having fun with them. And Luna and Bart, they're being nice?"

"Oh yeah," Olive says, "they're really nice people, Mom. I think it's funny though, being in a house with just one mom and one dad. I've never been in a house like this before."

"That's true," I say. "I guess I never thought of it like that."

The girls smile. "Yeah, we get you all to ourselves," Olive says, laughing.

"Lucky me," I say, thankful they are focusing on me and not the fact they spent most of their lives raised by two other sister wives as well. "I can't wait to be home and give you both big hugs. We're going to have a sleepover in my bed and have pancakes for dinner."

"But you hate breakfast for dinner," Olive says.

I smile, loving how well my girls know me. After we say our goodbyes, Luna comes on the phone.

"You hanging in there?"

"Pretty well," I say, "and the girls?"

"They seem okay. They're just dolls," she says. "Last night I had Kendall and Julia over with their kids, and it got a little bit wild here. So tonight we're going to keep it low key. We're going to put on a movie in a few minutes. I told them they could watch half of it before bed and then half of it tomorrow after school; is that okay?"

"Of course," I say, "I trust your judgment."

"And how are things going with the handsome detective?" Luna asks, lifting her eyebrows.

I laugh. "Oh my God, can we not?"

"Really? I know it's a stressful time, but be good to yourself. You deserve it, Grace."

"Thank you," I say as I notice the diner

door swing open. "Oh, I think he's coming back right now."

"Then I'll let you go," Luna says. "Give me a call tomorrow, but honestly, don't sweat things over here. Just go get that son of yours and come home."

We say goodbye and I end the call, tucking my phone back in my purse.

"How are the girls?" Boone asks, handing over paper bags filled with greasy diner food. He turns on the car, and we make our way to the motel.

"Everyone's good. I miss them though, a lot. I'm just realizing how I have never spent time away from them before, not like this. And after Ruthie was gone for those few nights and then me leaving again, it just feels like a lot."

"You've never left the girls ever, not even for one night, huh?" Boone asks, pulling his car into a parking spot at the motel.

"Nope, I guess it's one of the downsides of living in a cult. You don't really get date night or anniversary weekends away."

"You have a lot of catching up to do, don't you?"

My cheeks burn at the idea that I need to catch up with nights out and romantic week-ends. I don't want to read too much into his comment, but it's impossible not to. The way I feel when I'm with Boone is a way I've never felt before with anyone, ever.

Once we get inside our room, Boone and I sit down at the small table, each of us taking a chair, and open our boxes.

"The waitress let me buy a bottle of wine from her too."

"You bought a bottle of wine from a diner?" I ask, laughing.

"That's got to be a first, right?" He shrugs. "Eh, I thought it would pair well with our hamburgers and french fries. But mostly I was hoping it might help you relax so you could get a good night's sleep."

"Thank you. I could really use that," I say as he unscrews the wine bottle cap and fills two glasses with a light red wine. We inhale our burgers and fries, and I drink my glass of wine faster than I've ever drank a glass of wine before. "Oh my gosh, we never drank at Garden Temple, so I'm a bit of a lightweight," I say. "This is probably a bad idea."

"Which part?" he asks.

I laugh as he tops my glass off and his too.

"I'm not much of a drinker," I admit, "like, hardly ever."

"See? You are already making headway on this catching-up thing."

"When you said that earlier, what did you mean exactly? You really think I need to catch up on dates?"

He twists his lips. "I know I'm not the most suave guy out there," he says, "and it doesn't really seem like the time to make a move, you know: all things considered."

I nod slowly, wiping my lips with my napkin. "So if we weren't looking for my crazy cult leader husband and teenage son and his pregnant girlfriend, maybe we would be on a date or something?" I ask. "Like, if this was a different reality?"

Boone nods. "Well, definitely if it was a different reality."

I smile. "Yeah? So how would it have gone down in this alternate reality?" I ask, teasing the conversation out. "In a reality where you hadn't married your college sweetheart and I hadn't gotten married at fourteen, and neither of us had kids or marriages that fell apart." I rest my hand on my chin, propping my elbow on the table. "What would that alternate reality be like? Say we just met at the diner tonight for the first time."

Boone smiles sadly, leaning back in his

chair. "I *reckon*," he says, emphasizing the word, "that I would have put a quarter in the jukebox and asked you to dance."

I try not to grin; it's hard. "You dance?" I say, "I can't picture it. What song would you have chosen?"

"The song wouldn't have mattered," he says.

"What *would* have mattered?" I ask.

"My partner. You. The woman in my arms."

The motel room is quiet and still. The lighting is awful, and the furniture is dated, but the moment is ours. Boone's eyes lock with mine, and I swear we're in that diner all alone with the lights off and the music on, and his hips pressed against mine, my cheek on his chest, his hands holding mine.

I swallow. "Dance with me now?"

Boone doesn't speak. Instead, he stands and reaches for my hand, taking it in his. We don't need music. The songs of our hearts have been playing so loudly since the day we met, a constant beat, a thump, thump, thump, a rhythm that won't stop. A sound that stills me and soothes me, comforts me. A sound that steadies me in a way a song never has.

I hear his heartbeat, and I know he hears mine, and there are tears in my eyes for the magic of this moment that Boone is granting me. A wish I never knew I needed.

"Gray," he says, and he cups my cheek with his hand, and I close my eyes, tilting my head ever so slightly so that he cradles it. His other hand is wrapped around my waist, drawing me closer still. I lift my chin, my eyes on his, and he kisses me.

The kind of kiss that both grounds me and sweeps me away.

The kind of kiss I've been waiting for all of my life.

12

I SUPPOSE the kiss could turn into more, but when it ends, I step back.

"I don't know if it's strange to tell you this," I say. My voice cracks, my heart distinctly aware of how close Boone is to me. "But that kiss is not one I will forget. Ever."

Boone smiles, and it fills the room. My eyes brighten. And so do his. He kisses my forehead before stepping away. "You're something else, West," he says before cleaning up the boxes of our dinner.

"West?"

He shrugs. "You call me Boone. Besides, Gray is an alias."

"How do you know West isn't an alias too?"

Boone runs a hand over his jaw. "I looked up your parents' accident. You were always a West."

I swallow, feeling seen. "Gray doesn't feel like an alias anymore. It feels right."

"You really don't like the idea of being called West?"

I laugh. "My dad was a baseball coach for the high school where he taught. Coach West. I guess hearing it made me think of him."

"Is that a bad thing?" Boone asks.

"It's a painful thing."

"I won't do it again," Boone says. When I speak, this man listens. When I cry, he doesn't tell me to stop. When I need help, he asks how. He is no ordinary man.

If my life had been different, if my parents were still alive, he is the sort of man I would have been proud to bring home. He is the kind of man I want to share all of myself with.

I turn to him, needing to pull him close. Needing to kiss him again. My desire scares me, unnerves me. Takes my breath away.

"What?" Boone asks, moving toward me as I let out a sigh. The longing deep inside is more than I understand. But he understands it perfectly. Orion Boone understands me.

"You can call me anything you like," I whisper as his hands find my hips. "Just don't call me and say goodbye. I don't think I could handle it, Boone. Losing you."

"Gray West, I'm not going anywhere." His mouth finds mine again, and this time it's not a kiss that tiptoes around the depths of our hearts. It's a kiss that's already found the cave, a kiss that walks toward the dark, not needing a lantern. Because this kiss is filled entirely with light.

He runs his hands up my back, and I exhale at his tender touch. Wanting him closer still. I lift my sweater up over my head, needing Boone's calloused hands to run across my skin.

"You're beautiful," he whispers in my ear, and a tear falls down my cheek. Boone kisses it away. Kisses away all of my fears as we move to the bed. I unbutton his flannel shirt and he pulls me close.

"You aren't like other men," I say, my eyes closed, my heart his.

"And you aren't like other women." He traces his finger from my chin to my chest. I hold my breath, scared of missing a moment.

"I've never been with someone who saw me," I admit, my eyes now open, finding his.

"You want to be seen?" Boone cradles my body, gazing down. His strength carrying me past my inhibitions.

"I want to be seen by you."

We undress slowly, the motel room lighting offering a soft glow on a night that changes me from the inside out. We move as one, finding a rhythm all our own. I don't carry any insecurities with me into this moment. Instead, I offer him the parts of myself I've kept hidden, locked away, for so long.

His words are soft and sincere, his body against mine solid as a rock, and I know he won't break me. I've always wanted a man to care for me. But I doubted I was worthy of that kind of care. Boone holds me like I am something special. Like I am his.

————

When I wake in the morning, I'm shocked to see it's after seven thirty. I check my phone, but there are no messages.

Boone is still sleeping too, his arm around my bare body. I'm nestled against him, my back to his chest. I blink, realizing that sleeping all night in the same bed with a man is a novel thing.

When I slept with Jeremiah, it was transactional. He would come to me; he would get what he needed, and he would leave. We'd never wake up in the same bed.

My body warms at the thought of where I am now, but the new day brings a focus I need to remember. I need to speak with Genevieve. And time is not on our side.

I head to the bathroom to brush my teeth and get dressed. When I reemerge, Boone is pulling on clean clothes too.

"You sleep okay?" he asks, looking at me with new eyes. This is all new territory. After last night, things between us are undoubtedly different.

"Yes, but now ..."

"Coffee?" Boone finishes my sentence. Not mentioning last night, his body next to mine.

I nod. "Exactly. Coffee."

We put our luggage in the trunk of his car, neither of us wanting to imagine another night here without being closer to the truth—closer to finding my son.

At the diner, we order quickly. While we're waiting for the food to be delivered, I call Genevieve again. This time she picks up.

"Grace?" she asks. "I got your voice mail last night, but I didn't want to call you back. I thought it'd be too late. I was going to call you this morning, but didn't know when it would be too early."

"No, no, it's fine," I say. "Don't explain. I'm just glad you picked up."

"Yeah. It's so weird you called," she says.

"Really? Why?"

"I've been thinking about the past a lot recently."

"Can I come see you?" I ask. "I'm over at Moses Lake."

"I live in Ritzville," she says, "but do you want to meet halfway? There's a coffee shop in Troutdale. I could be there in half an hour."

"Perfect," I say. We end the call.

It's so strange hearing her voice. But it's not just her voice that feels bizarre. It's the fact that she's alive when I thought she was dead.

The food arrives as I explain the plan to Boone. He pulls out cash from his wallet and sets it on the table, taking one bite of hash browns before standing.

I frown. "I feel bad leaving before we've eaten."

He shakes his head. "No, this is more important. Come on. We don't want to miss her."

"I don't think she would leave without talking to us."

"Gray, we can't waste an opportunity like this. Come on."

Thirty minutes later, we pull into the coffee shop in Troutdale. There are a few cars in the lot, and we step inside. I spot her immediately, a latte in front of her on the table.

Genevieve has curly red hair and pale-blue eyes, and skin that is covered in freckles. I was always envious of it. It looks like she is covered in sunshine. She stands upon seeing me. She's in a long, flowy skirt with a scarf around her neck. No makeup on her face, yet she looks ethereal, angelic.

"Grace!" she says. "Look at you!"

I laugh, looking down at myself in blue jeans and a purple sweater. "Yeah, I suppose I do look different."

"Your hair!" she says, reaching for my short locks. "I can't believe it. Your braid was down your back." She smiles brightly, and I remember why I liked her so much. She has that warm, effervescent personality that just draws you to her.

A magic quality, a quality Jeremiah wanted, but his was always a tad forced. And I only knew that because I knew him so well. But Genevieve's warmth? It's all natural.

"Hi," she says, sticking out her hand to Boone. "I'm Genevieve. And you are?"

"Orion," he says. "I'm a friend of Grace's."

"Well, great to meet you. Do you want to get something to drink?"

"Sure. I'll go order," he says.

I smile, thanking him, and sit down with Genevieve. "What have you been up to," I ask her, "since you *left*?"

She laughs. "It sounds like that's the question."

"Did you leave?" I ask. "Or did something happen?"

"Oh, I didn't leave on my own accord," she says. "Jeremiah basically drove me to the middle of nowhere and kicked me out of the car."

"Seriously?"

"What did you think happened?"

I lick my lips, telling her the truth. She covers her mouth, shocked, when I finish explaining.

Boone sits down and hands me my cup of coffee and a breakfast sandwich. Across from me, Genevieve is drinking green tea and eating a bran muffin.

"He told you I died in a car crash?" she asks. "Pretty low blow considering I slept with him."

At that, my eyebrows raise.

She groans. "Oh my gosh. I probably shouldn't have said that." She gives me a cringe. "I slept with Jeremiah, which I kind of feel bad about, but kind of not. I don't know. Everything that happened at Garden Temple was so weird. When did you leave?"

I swallow. Her casual tone about the whole situation unnerves me. It's flippant in a way that I'm not ready for. "I left a year ago with my girls. Abel stayed, but recently we reconnected. Problem is, I think he's back there with his father now."

"You think?" she says. "I thought you were just at Moses Lake. You didn't see him?"

At that, I decide to lay out all my cards. I explain to her the entirety of the situation because there's no reason to hold back. I want her to trust me, to trust my story. So I tell her about Jeremiah and Bethany, about the voice mail and Eden, the empty compound, the bunkers, all of it.

"Oh my God," she says when I finish.

Boone is sitting there quietly the whole time, letting me take control of the situation, and I appreciate that.

"Where do you think they are?" Genevieve asks.

"I don't know," I admit. "That's why I called you. Your name was on a piece of paper listing all of the members of the congregation who had left. Dissenters. And so I thought maybe you might know something I don't. You might remember something Jeremiah told you about another place that he could have taken them."

Genevieve shakes her head. "I wouldn't know anything you don't know. I mean, you were his wife, his *first* wife." She looks over at Boone. "Grace was the woman everyone wanted to be," she says with a playful smirk. "I mean, look at her. She's like, ridiculously gorgeous, for one. And the fact she wore flour-sack dresses and her hair in a braid didn't take away her beauty."

Boone gives her a half smile, and I wonder what her description of me makes him think.

"But it wasn't just the way Grace looked that had everyone in awe. It was the way Jeremiah *looked at her.* It was what everybody else wanted, craved. His attention."

I shake my head. "Jeremiah hated me more than he liked me."

"I don't think that's quite right," Genevieve

says with a laugh. "Jeremiah was scared of you. Jealous of you."

While I don't see myself in the same way at all, I want to stick to Jeremiah. "Why did he kick you out?" I ask, deflecting the conversation from me. "Why did he want you to leave Garden Temple?"

Genevieve rolls her eyes. "He wanted more than a one-night stand." She shrugs. "I mean, I suppose that's the best way to put it. He wanted me to marry him and I said no."

"Why?" I ask.

"This is going to sound bad," she says, "but I didn't want to play third fiddle in your marriage. I would have married Jeremiah, but I wanted to be his first wife. I wasn't playing for seconds or thirds."

"This was before Naomi married him?" Boone asks.

I nod. "Right before, actually. He married Naomi quickly after you died. I mean, after you were taken away."

"Not surprised. I refused him, so he went and found someone younger and more willing."

"I had no idea," I say, stunned.

"I'm sorry." she says. "I shouldn't have slept

with him that one time, but you know how he is."

"Unfortunately, I do know how he is."

"And he's vindictive," Genevieve adds. "If he wasn't going to have me, no one could. So, he made me leave. Best thing that ever happened to me, actually."

"What do you mean?" I ask.

Genevieve shrugs, pulling apart her muffin. "I only joined the church because I was broke and in a bad place personally. When I met Jeremiah at an outreach event, he told me I was welcome to come to Garden Temple, which I did. And after I was kicked out, I reached out to a cousin of mine out in Ritzville. She told me I could stay with her until I got my life together. One of her room-mates was Bob, who is the love of my life." She flings her hand across the table, and on her ring finger, there's a modest diamond, an engagement ring. "We're getting married this summer. And I feel like the luckiest person in the world."

"Congratulations," I say, honestly happy for her. She dodged the biggest bullet of her life by not binding herself to Jeremiah. "What do you do in Ritzville?"

She smiles. "Crazily enough, I've been

training to be a yoga teacher. I've been practicing for a few years and I love it."

I smile, thinking of Luna's comment the other day, telling me I should take a yoga class with her.

"It changed my life," Genevieve says. "I feel centered and more grounded than I ever have before. I've been working with an energy healer on finding closure with my past, and that's why you've been on my mind. I've been wondering what happened with you. And then you called." She smiles warmly. "Like it was meant to be. And having Bob now, it just makes me feel like I can move on."

"That's really wonderful," I say, wondering how it would feel to truly find closure from Garden Temple. It feels so far out of reach.

Boone clears his throat. "Congratulations," he says. "But what you said earlier about Jeremiah being vindictive, what did you mean by that?"

Genevieve lifts her eyebrows. "Right. That's just his personality. Like, if he didn't get what he wanted, nobody else would either. You know what I mean?"

I nod. "Jeremiah was like an angry toddler. It was his way or the highway, and he made sure everybody knew that."

"Yeah, and he did more than send me to the highway, apparently. He killed me there too," Genevieve says with a wry laugh.

Boone and I look at one another. We're not smiling.

The truth is, Jeremiah is a dangerous man, and Genevieve's story just confirms that he is diabolical.

13

GENEVIEVE GIVES me a big hug goodbye. "I'm so glad you reached out and called me. I wish I could have helped more than I did."

"I'm just happy to see your face, to know that things are going so well for you," I tell her. "I can't believe we had a funeral for you."

"Jeremiah sure knew how to weave a story. We're better off without him, aren't we?"

I nod, knowing we definitely are.

"And I'm sending you a wedding invite, okay? You better come. And bring your whole family, Abel included. Heck, Bethany too. Hey, you can even bring this detective as your plus one," she says, elbowing Boone playfully. "I mean it though. I've got to see you again under happier circumstances."

"You think I'll find him before it's too late?" I ask.

She nods. "I know it might be a little woo-woo, but since I'm into meditation and all that shit, I'm telling you I'm sending all the positive vibes into the universe today. And I need you to call me when this is all over, when you've got your boy back home, okay? Let me know that everything went okay."

"I like how you're not taking no for an answer."

"I'm not. Hell, I already had to die for Jeremiah. I'm not letting anyone else die for that man."

After she leaves, Boone and I get into his car and we sit in the parking lot.

"What now?" I ask. "The compound again?"

Boone nods. "That's what I was thinking. And we can call Charlie if we don't find any leads."

On our way out of Troutdale, we pull over at a rest stop. I step into the bathroom and splash cold water on my face, trying to collect my thoughts. It's been an emotional day and I'm wrung out. Drying my face and hands with a paper towel, I look in the mirror, feeling so weathered, so worn out and aged. I'm thirty years old and feel like I've lived a thousand life-

times, half of them in the last week. The fluorescent lighting isn't doing anything for the
circles under my eyes, and my hair's gone limp,
tired just like me.

Back in the parking lot, Boone holds up a
few packages of trail mix and bottle of water he
grabbed from a vending machine. "You ready
to go?"

I nod. "Yes. And thank you."

"For what?" he asks as we walk out to
his car.

"For being here, for putting up with all of
this. I said I didn't want to go on a wild-goose
chase, but that's exactly what it feels like,
doesn't it?"

"Hey," he says, "don't apologize for
anything, and don't thank me either. I want to
be here for you."

Back in the car, with the music turned
down low, we eat as we drive. "I do this all the
time," he says, "eat in my car."

"Really?" I ask. "Not me. I always pack my
lunch for work and eat in the break room."

"You like working at the library?" he asks.

"I do, but I especially love the hours. I don't
work weekends, so I never need to pay for
childcare."

"You plan on being there a long time?"

"Maybe. Did I ever tell you how I wanted to be a florist when I was little?"

"Why is that?"

I tell him how my dad would always buy my mom bouquets of flowers for no good reason, how I always thought they not only made the house seem prettier, but they put my mom in a good mood.

"Jeremiah ever buy you flowers?" he asks.

"Not once."

"Okay. So you didn't celebrate anniversaries or anything like that?"

I shake my head. "No, but since we're getting personal, what about you and your ex-wife? Did you buy her flowers?"

Boone scoffs. "She was not the type to want flowers."

"I didn't realize there was such a type," I say between bites of trail mix.

"There is," he says, looking over at me. "She wasn't that kind of woman."

"*That kind of woman* sounds a little condescending," I point out.

"I don't mean it like that. I mean she wouldn't have appreciated much sentimentality. She wasn't into romantic gestures."

"Did that cramp your style?" I ask.

Boone shrugs, looking over at me. "You really want to go there?" he asks.

"Maybe," I say. "I feel like you know everything about me, and I don't know much about you."

"Ex-wives can be complicated territory."

"*I* am complicated territory," I say. "I promise you, that ex-wife of yours has nothing on me."

Boone laughs then, and the sound of his laughter fills up the car, opens my heart in a way that I need. I need the light to come in somehow, and I appreciate Boone's ability to do that in the middle of a very tense situation.

"The truth is we have a car ride in front of us, and dwelling on the fact that my family is fractured won't help us get to the compound any faster," I tell him. "It might be good to get our mind off Jeremiah for a moment." I pause. "So what was Leanne like?"

He looks over at me again, one eye on the road. "I didn't know you knew her name."

"Charlie told me," I admit.

Boone smirks. "That sounds about right."

"So, she was a police officer," I say.

Boone nods very slowly. "She still is. She works in Seattle."

"Did you guys used to be on the same

beat?" I ask, having no idea if that is the correct lingo.

"We met at the academy. She's really good at her job, but wasn't so good at relationships."

"So she was the problem?" I ask.

He shakes his head. "We were together before we knew what we really wanted. Sure, we were both starting our careers, but we were never really on the same page about what we wanted. We fell into a relationship that turned into a marriage. And after Suzanne"—Boone shakes his head—"I'm not saying she was the straw that broke the camel's back because that sounds a little crass, but Leanne and I were never going to last anyway. It just forced the end sooner than either of us were expecting. And now she's dating a woman, so," Boone chuckles. "Honestly, we were doomed from the beginning."

"Really?" I say. "So she's ..."

"Gay," Boone fills in. "Yeah."

"Did you know?"

Boone shakes his head. "I don't know. Like I said, Leanne kept her cards close to the chest, and we were better friends than anything else. Better friends than lovers, I guess you could say. We were good parents, good partners. We got along."

"Do you still?" I ask.

Boone runs a hand over his temple. "Well enough. We shared a life together, and we both loved Suzanne with all that we were. So I figure we'll always be connected in some ways."

"That makes sense," I say. "I wish I had no connection to Jeremiah. I love my kids, but I hate that he is their father."

Boone gets quiet, brings his latte to his lips and takes a drink. When he sets it back down in the cup holder, he clears his throat. "You and Jeremiah are a bit more complicated than Leanne and I ever were. I respect Leanne. We weren't destined for some happily ever after in our old age, but I care for her. I want her to be happy. She's a good woman. She just wasn't my woman. But Jeremiah, he's a criminal, a rapist. He very well may be a murderer."

"He is, but do you think they'll be able to make him pay?" I ask.

Boone shrugs. "I don't know how this will all play out, but he's manipulated people into giving him their money, their property, their entire lives. There are consequences to that. So sure, you and Jeremiah brought children into this world together, but it doesn't mean Jeremiah has to have a part in your future, Gray."

"I know," I say, "and I don't want him to. I

just want this whole thing to be done with once and for all."

"So that you can go learn to be a florist?" he asks with a smile.

I shake my head. "No, I don't want that dream anymore."

"What do you want?" he asks.

I lick my lips. I think of my children, what my life was like when they were young. How scared and alone I felt. When I'm very honest with myself, what I want is to have a child with a man who loves me and cares for me, protects me and supports me, and to raise that child in a safe and happy home. But I can't tell Boone that. That feels too raw, too real to share with a man who I admire so deeply.

"What," Boone says, "no big dreams for your future?"

I exhale. "I read once that it's hard to have dreams when you're in survival mode, and it really made sense to me, you know? I've been so busy fighting my whole life to just get through it that I haven't had a lot of time to just sit back and imagine what my life could be, to dream about a future."

"I get that," Boone says. "And I hope one day you do get that chance, to sit on your porch and look up at the sky and think about what you really want. Without the fear of Jeremiah or even the smaller fears of paying your bills and getting your rent in on time. That you can start imagining years and decades of your life spread out in front of you."

"Thanks, Boone," I say. "That's a really nice thing to say."

"I mean it," he says, "I want you to be happy, Gray."

"Why do you care so much about me?" I ask, and I know I'm fishing. But right now, after the morning I've had, I don't think it's the worst thing to want to feel good.

"Because sometimes when I look at you"—Boone shakes his head—"that future we were talking about? I see it."

The silence that fills the car after that is not a dangerous quiet. The silence is filled with a tender kind of hope, the kind I've longed for all my life.

I might not be sitting out on my porch, looking at the sky, but I allow myself to imagine, to dream.

And with Boone beside me, it does feel right.

14

"HEY, WAIT," I say when we're halfway to the compound. "That convenience store to the left, pull in there."

"Sure, what's up?"

"I remember Abel talking about this place. It's where he got his phone. He said sometimes on the way back from the construction site they would stop here, at Handy's Pit Stop. Maybe Handy knows where they went."

He nods. "Yes, let's go in and ask. They might know something."

Inside the gas station, I optimistically take out my phone, pulling up a photograph of Abel. I hold my phone in my hand, scared to speak, but when the man behind the register asks how he can help, I tell him the truth.

"I'm looking for my son; his name's Abel. He's almost sixteen. He lives down at the compound that's not too far from here. They have a construction crew, Garden Construction," I say with a lift in my voice. "Anyway, I know that they stop here sometimes after work, and I thought maybe you might recognize him. He's missing."

The man frowns. "Do you have a picture?"

"Yes," I say. "Yes, of course." I turn my phone to face him. "I know he's been in here. He bought some flip phones from you and ..."

"I know that kid, yeah. He'd come in here sometimes, buy chips and soda. He got some phones. He's your boy?"

I nod. "Yes, Abel Priest."

The man runs a hand over his jaw. "They usually come in early in the morning like this, or right before dinner. They stop here, get gas, pick up a few things. Kind of quiet group of men."

"Yes, that is probably right. They kept to themselves."

"I hear them talk sometimes. They've been working over on Pack Mile Road. I thought it was a construction site, but my buddy Eric, he was up there hunting a few weeks ago, and he said there's this whole maze of containers underground. Looked like they were building an underground bunker."

My voice falters, "Underground?"

"Yeah, it's kind of crazy, right? Anyway, I've never been out there myself, but you want me to give my buddy a call?"

"Pack Mile Road near here?" Boone asks.

"Yeah, only about twenty minutes east. They have some real nice trails out there. My friend got himself a five-point buck, if you believe it."

"Oh, I believe it," Boone says warmly, somehow fitting in with this man. "Well, that's good to know. Maybe they're out there now."

"Maybe," the guy says, "but I haven't seen them this morning. I haven't actually seen them the last few days, which is kind of weird. Sometimes they stop and get beer and shit, and I always think, 'Man, it's early in the morning to be drinking a sixteen ouncer.'"

Boone chuckles. "Yeah, they must be working hard if they're building a bunker."

"Exactly," the guy says. "Anyway, sorry I don't know anymore. But they weren't, like, mean guys; they just kind of seemed serious. And your kid," he says, pointing back to my phone, "he never wanted anyone to see what he was buying. He'd always be the last to leave. It made me kind of laugh. That's kind of how I was when I was a kid."

I smile tightly. "Right. I probably was the same too. Wouldn't have wanted my parents to know what I was up to if it was no good. Thanks," I say.

"Sure. You know where you're going?"

Boone nods, rapping his knuckles on the counter. "Yep, Pack Mile Road. Appreciate it."

"Good luck, man," the guy calls as we leave.

In the car, I look over at Boone. "Well, that was easy."

"Is that what we're calling it?" He snorts. "What were they doing out there on Pack Mile?"

"They were planning on going to Eden. They were building something for the congregation. I'm guessing that's it."

"You think they're there right now?" he asks.

I swallow. "Maybe. It makes sense. They're not at the lodge, so maybe this is the religious retreat. The bunker is Eden. I knew they were working on something, and I suppose I knew Eden was a physical location. I just ..."

"What?" Boone asks.

I shrug. "It's just crazy if they were working on some sort of underground shelter, and none of the women knew this whole time."

"Why didn't you ask?" he asks.

"We weren't allowed to ask questions like that," I tell Boone, tense. "I wish you understood what it was like, but at the same time, I actually don't. Martindale is a chauvinist pig, but all the men I grew up with are like that. Boone, I was fourteen when Jeremiah made me his wife, so I know a thing or two about unkind men. Martindale is not the worst of them. But the men at this underground shelter, they *are* the worst of them, and if they're all there and it's us against them, we don't stand a chance."

"I'll take care of you," he says.

"I'm not doubting that, but two against two hundred? We need backup. We need more help."

"We don't have it," Boone says. "You heard the people at Grant County; they're not interested in helping us. That police station is in the Middle Ages."

"I know. I just feel like we're going to put ourselves in a really dangerous situation really quickly."

"Do you want to stop?" he asks. "Do you want to pretend we never heard that information at the convenience store and drive back to

Tacoma and say we gave it our best college try? Because those are our choices right now, Gray. This is when you put up or shut up."

"I'm not going to shut up. I'm going to fight for my child."

"Exactly," Boone says, "that's why we're going out to Pack Mile Road. We're going to figure out what the hell is going on."

"You're right." I exhale, clinging to the plan. "I just got scared."

"It's okay to be scared. You just can't give in to it completely," Boone says.

"I don't want anything bad to happen."

Boone reaches for my hand and squeezes it. "Gray, neither do I."

15

As we pull onto Pack Mile Road, I admit to feeling a sense of hope. Of course I don't want them to be here, having done something terrible. But I do want them to be here. I want answers, and I know we don't have time for a wild-goose chase across the state.

"There's a bunch of trucks over there," Boone says, pointing through the window. "Looks like an outbuilding or two and a big backhoe." There are massive piles of dirt next to the outbuilding that Boone points to, and as he pulls up to it, I see a few vans and trucks with the Garden Construction logo on the sides.

"This must be it," I say as we park the car

and get out. "But there's not enough cars here for this to be the entire congregation," I say.

"I know," Boone says, running a hand over his jaw. "Shit. I was really hoping it would be as simple as that. We'd show up here. We'd find them. We put an end to their madness." Boone kicks at a rock. I zip my coat up to my neck, ready to start moving toward the buildings, wanting to find the bunker that the man working at Handy's Pit Stop mentioned.

"We might as well get a closer look. Maybe someone's here, or maybe we can get a clue."

"A clue, huh?" Boone says, shaking his head, clearly discouraged. "What was Jeremiah's endgame?" he asks, looking up to the sky.

I'm thankful it's blue skies and clear. I learned, after last weekend's snow and rainstorms, how weather can play a part in getting to the bottom of things, how it can stop an investigation. Not that this is anything formal like that, but it's still up to us to figure out where Abel went.

"Jeremiah's endgame? I don't know for certain, but his priority was pretty simple," I say, walking toward the outbuilding. Boone follows.

"Simple, how?" he asks.

"All Jeremiah wanted or cared about was

allegiance. He wanted absolute devotion, and he has it from everyone but me."

"You think he's trying to get back at you?"

"Not necessarily *back* at me, but he wants to prove to his followers that his word is as good as God's. He wants their devotion in life and in death. He will stop at nothing to ensure it," I say.

"You knew this while you were there?"

"What do you know about living in a cult like this?" I ask Boone as I pull back the door to the outbuilding. I flip on a light switch that miraculously works, and inside, there are shovels, bags of gravel, spools of electrical wiring. There are shelves of random supplies, but no people.

"I don't know anything about living in a cult," Boone says, moving bags of concrete around, looking for something—anything—that might point us in a new direction. "I'm just here trying to help you, Gray."

"Did you ever go to church growing up?" I ask. "Do you believe in God?"

"Not really," he says. "It wasn't like my parents were atheists, but we also weren't churchgoers. I remember when I was little, some years my grandma would have us dress up and go to church with her on Easter and

Christmas Eve, but none of us were devout by any means."

"Have you ever experienced a situation where people pledge their allegiance to the leader, the person in charge?"

"I guess the closest would be when I played college ball."

"You went to college?"

"Yeah," he says. "I went to Eastern Washington University. Played football."

"What was your degree in?" I ask him, walking around the dirt floor of the outbuilding. They didn't take much time building this place.

"Criminal law."

I frown. "Why didn't you become a lawyer?"

"It wasn't for me. I never took the bar. I realized I could either spend my days in a courthouse or spend them on the streets. I figured I might be better suited for hunting down the bad guys than defending them."

"That's interesting," I say. "But I'm not surprised."

"No? Why is that?" he asks as we walk out of the building, closing the door.

"I just can't exactly picture you in a suit and tie in front of a judge."

"You've seen me in a suit."

I laugh. "You wear suits very poorly," I tell him. "Every one I've seen you in was so wrinkled, it needed to be taken to the dry cleaners."

"Wow. Tell me how you really feel. Here I was thinking we were getting somewhere."

I laugh. "Boone, that's not what I was trying to get at. I like you. I just don't picture you going to a law office. I can't see it."

"I was top of my class," he says, defending himself.

"Wow, I'm impressed."

Outside, we walk around the large piles of dirt, indicating that there are massive holes dug out somewhere. We walk toward them, and that's when we see what the guy at Handy's Pit Stop was referring to. A dozen shipping containers are shaped into a rectangle twenty feet down. There is no evidence of people, no trash, no signs of life. There is a ladder leading to the pit, and a crooked wooden sign above an entrance on a shipping container that's painted in green: *EDEN: Eternity Is Waiting.*

If this is Jeremiah's idea of Eden, it is a disappointment. This is no paradise.

Boone has a hand over his eyes, shielding the bright morning sun. But I don't want to cover my eyes. I want to see all of this. Every last detail.

I need to see what is in the containers down there. I need to know what the men I lived with were building.

Boone has the idea to look through one of the forgotten vans to see if there are any flashlights, and we get lucky. There are several. We each take one and then climb down the ladder that's propped on the edge of the big pit. Boone goes first, and then I follow. When we get to the bottom of the pit, we look around.

The containers remind me of last week when I was hellbent on finding Ruthie. Our neighbor Cory was a suspect, and he had an old shipping container by the railroad tracks that he used as his bunker. His was more of a hideout for selling drugs and wreaking havoc. This place is different. This place has darker roots, deadlier connotations.

"It's not what I think of when I think of the Garden of Eden," Boone says, clapping his hands against one of the rusty-green metal walls of the container.

"Me neither. I always pictured some hippie commune paradise with a bunch of yurts and flowers in our hair, and this isn't that."

"No," he says. "It isn't." He looks at a lock and chain on one of the containers. "Damn, I need a bolt cutter."

"Maybe there's one in the van," I suggest. Boone nods.

"You stay here. I'll be right back."

"Okay." He jogs over to the ladder, and a minute later, he's out of sight. I walk around the shipping containers, trying to imagine what Jeremiah was thinking when he put these here, how much it cost to buy these and drop them down. My skin crawls at the thought of what's inside. I'm honestly scared to know.

When Boone returns, he has nothing in his hands.

"There's nothing that would cut through that metal," he says.

"I wasn't getting my hopes up," I say, reaching for the chain and the lock that binds it.

Jeremiah may have been smart about some things, but apparently he was a little cocky about others. Too certain that no one would trespass him, but here I am entering the digits to our anniversary once more.

Boone's eyes narrow. "So, your wedding meant a lot to him, huh? Why was that?"

"Well, in part, I was this young, very young woman, so there was some sort of sick fantasy that must've come along with that," I say, undoing the chain from the door. I hold the lock in my hand and drop the chain to the ground. "But it also marked a change in the way Jeremiah led Garden Temple. For a long time, there was this whole power given to celibacy, but then he decided to take me as a wife to save me from a situation," I say, glossing over the truth.

Boone doesn't ask me what I mean by situation, so I keep going. "Marrying me marked the beginning of Jeremiah's role as a husband, a different kind of leader, and when he married Lydia and then Naomi, it gave a message to the other men in the congregation that they, too, could take multiple wives. So, suddenly, there was this power structure that wasn't really there in the beginning."

I look at Boone to gauge his reaction to my explanation. He gives nothing away with his expression, and I realize that is a skill that must come in handy as a detective. The ability to mask one's emotions, to hear a story without weighing in.

I continue to explain, "At first, at Garden Temple, men were at the head of the household and had command over the women, but it was more in a traditional sense. But suddenly the men had control over multiple women who were submitting to them. The more wives a man took, the more power he held, and Jeremiah used that as a part of his ideology. He preached that God had given men a capacity that women didn't have. The husbands became more powerful, and the wives became submissive, and that worked for Jeremiah. It's worked for all sorts of groups of men throughout time. And there were three times as many women at Garden Temple because Jeremiah found them at women's shelters or at prayer meetings, women who were desperate. Who needed a way out. He tricked them by offering a lifeline when they needed it most.

"The hardest part for me," I explain, "is what it means for the young girls who were growing up there, girls like Olive and Ruthie. I couldn't let what happened to me happen to them. I couldn't. Jeremiah taking me as his wife was the downfall of Garden Temple. It turned us from conservative Christians to fundamentally flawed followers, and there was no going back from it."

"You blame yourself?" Boone asks.

"Yes, I blame myself. I blame myself because"—I blink back tears at this, the truth, so close—"if I would've made a different decision, everything might have ended differently."

"What do you mean, different decision?"

Boone says. "I thought Jeremiah wanted you, picked you out to be his wife."

I shake my head. "No, Boone. That's not really how it happened. What happened was I was supposed to marry Bishop Timothy, and I couldn't stand the idea of it. He was going to rape me, and I wouldn't let him. I killed him. And Jeremiah knew. He married me to cover up the murder."

16

"What do you mean?" Boone asks.

I turn my back to him and pull open the door of the bunker, not wanting to meet his eyes. Wanting the distraction of this terrifying underground building that Jeremiah built with the other men at Garden Temple.

I flip on a light, but it doesn't work. There's no electricity down here. We turn on our flashlights, and the space lights up. I wish I were still in the dark. Telling Boone my secrets is no easy thing.

"Gray, are you going to answer me?" Boone asks.

I don't know what to say, how to say it.

"Gray," he says louder now, "look at me."

"What do you want me to say?" I ask,

turning to him. Our eyes adjusting to the strange lighting. It's dim, dark, but I can make out his face, and I know he can make out mine. There are several couches down here. A coffee table, a log-in book of some sort on a table with a pen. It looks like a meeting room, with a dozen chairs.

"You want me to tell you the whole ugly truth?" I ask.

"Yes," he says, "I do."

"You won't ever be able to look at me the same way," I tell him, stepping closer.

"How do you want me to look at you, Gray?"

"I don't know," I say, my voice caught in my throat, scared. "But it will be different than the way you look at me now."

Boone doesn't give in to my fear though. "Tell me what you meant when you said you killed a man."

"It's exactly that," I tell him, shivering from the cold down here, in this half-made house my husband built. "I was supposed to marry Bishop Timothy, but he was a bad man. The way he looked at me ... he was four times my age, maybe five. My uncle, he hadn't died yet, and he gave this man permission to marry me. Bishop Timothy's wife had died and he was alone. He wanted a wife. He wanted me. So, my uncle agreed, gave him my hand, and Jeremiah gave him his blessing. I figured out why years later," I tell Boone, sitting down on a couch, the weight of this story making it hard to stand.

Boone sits next to me. "What did you figure out?"

I turn to him. "I figured out why Jeremiah and my uncle were okay with this old man marrying such a young girl. Bishop Timothy was rich. He had a lot of money, and he donated it to Garden Temple. His first wife was an heiress, and after she passed, Bishop Timothy became a very wealthy man." I look around the bunker, shaking my head. "He probably funded this entire project. So Jeremiah wanted him to stay, to remain happy, satisfied. Jeremiah wanted to give him what he wanted because it meant Jeremiah's pockets were filled. That mattered a lot in those days when Jeremiah was still so new at this, at being a prophet to so many people. So in exchange for his money, Jeremiah offered him me, a child," I say, the words leaving my mouth sounding disgusting, grotesque. True.

"So what happened?" Boone asks, his emotions no longer concealed. It's like he sees the angry heartbreak in my eyes and matches it with his own rage. "Did you marry him?"

The look in Boone's eyes is so disturbed that I have to look away because it makes me ashamed of myself. I feel dirty. I feel vulnerable. I feel like I would rather be anywhere else in the world than in this underground bunker with a man whose respect for me is fading, fast.

"We were set to marry," I tell Boone. "The day before, I had one chance. I was standing with Bishop Timothy in Jeremiah's office. We were alone and he came close. So close. I knew he was going to touch me, do things to me that scared me. He stepped forward and drew me to him. He told me what he planned on doing to me on our wedding night. He said, why wait? He reached for the hem of my dress, and his hands ... they slid up my thigh ... and I lost it. Or maybe I gained control for the first time since my parents died.

"I reached behind me and grabbed a paperweight from Jeremiah's desk and smashed it over his head. He fell back, his head hit the bookshelf. He bled out on the floor. The blow was fatal. After he crashed to the floor, I dropped to my knees, horrified, but also completely relieved. If he was dead, it meant I didn't have to marry him.

"Jeremiah rushed into the room, and he saw the blood on the floor, the blood in my hands. He knew what I'd done. The paperweight in front of me. But Jeremiah didn't condemn me; he didn't shame me. He helped me." I press my lips together, remembering that day so vividly. Jeremiah was my knight in shining armor. My savior. "After the bishop had taken his last breath—there was no saving him —Jeremiah made me a promise in that room. Jeremiah told me he had been given a revelation from God in that very moment. A vision. God had told him what to do," I say, remembering how Jeremiah had cupped my cheek and pushed back my hair and looked at me. Now, I lift my chin, eyes filled with tears that run down my cheeks. Boone reaches out, and he takes my hand to steady me. He doesn't let go.

"Gray," he says, "it's okay."

I shake my head. "It's not okay. I was relieved, Boone. I was happy. I *wanted* to marry Jeremiah. I knew I would be required to sleep with Jeremiah too, but it wasn't a scary proposition; he was the prophet, and it was God's decree. I felt chosen, and believed God had actually answered my prayers. I was delusional. I thought Jeremiah really did hear something from his Heavenly Father because that's what I wanted to believe. And that's why, even now, when I think about all of those people who followed Jeremiah to God knows where, I can understand them. When you're desperate for something to be true, you let it become your story. I was desperate to get out of that marriage to Bishop Timothy, and Jeremiah gave me a way out. He gave me hope. I gladly took what he offered. And look at what it's cost all of us."

"It's not your fault," Boone says. "Gray, listen to me; it's not your fault."

"What isn't?" I say. "If I hadn't killed that man, Jeremiah would have never taken a wife. He would have never let the men become so powerful at Garden Temple, and he wouldn't be so mad that I left. So..." I say, my shoulders lifting and falling, "that's the truth. I'm a killer. I killed a man. And because of that, many more may die."

Boone holds my hand tight. "Gray, I remember after Elle died, putting an end to the whole wELLEness Center disaster, you asked me about self-defense. Is this why? You wanted to know if you would be convicted for something you did as a child to a man who intended to rape you?"

I nod. "Jeremiah knew I was unhappy later in our marriage when the fantasy faded. So he held the bishop's murder over me. He told me he would go to the authorities and turn me in as a killer. He said he kept evidence—the paperweight with Bishop Timothy's blood, my fingerprints. And I thought that would be enough to convict me of something. It never entered my mind that that evidence would also show how Jeremiah had covered it up. I thought Jeremiah's word was stronger than mine, so I let it become the song in my head that was on repeat, a tune I couldn't get rid of."

"Now you know though," Boone says. "You know it's not your fault. That you're not a killer. Not like that."

"Not like what?" I say.

"It was self-defense," Boone says.

"Sure," I say. "But all I can wonder now is, was it worth it? Was saving myself worth the price of so many other lives?" I lick my lips, shake my head.

"I think you're worth a hell of a lot more than you think you are."

I close my eyes. I squeeze them shut, tight. Still, the tears escape, streaming down my cheeks, and my chin quivers as I cry.

I cry for the girl I lost after my parents died.

I cry for the girl who ended up here, under Jeremiah's thumb for so, so long.

Boone's hand is on my back, and he doesn't tell me to stop or to be quiet or that it's all right because he seems to know that it's not. None of this is all right, and the terrifying truth is maybe it will never be, because I'm no closer to finding Bethany and Abel than I was two days ago.

The clock's not just ticking, it might've already run out.

17

WHEN I FINALLY FINISH CRYING, we stand. "Thank you," I tell Boone, "for listening."

He looks down at me, and for a moment, I think he might kiss me. After all, last night he did so much more.

But he doesn't. Instead, Boone gives me a hug. A big, long hug. A hug that squeezes me tight until I can't breathe, until I'm laughing, telling him to let go. And he laughs too, looking down at me. "Those kinds of hugs always make things better," he tells me.

When he smiles, I see his left cheek dimple. And I feel like he's the best kind of teddy bear. The kind that comforts you when you're sad, that you want to take everywhere you go. "I think that was the best hug I've ever had," I admit, wiping my face with my palms, smoothing down my hair.

"Good," Boone says, "We all have our superpowers, you know. I can't wait to find out what yours is."

I smile. "Then let's start looking, and maybe you'll find out."

With our flashlights in hand, we begin to walk through the maze of interconnected bunkers. Considering all the time the men from Garden Temple spent here, I assumed it would be complete, but it's not even close. While the bunkers are pretty well cleaned, there is nothing much here. It is certainly not ready for the congregation to move into.

Several bunkers have bunk beds built in them, but no mattresses, no bedding. One has nothing but a few wooden dressers. Another bunker holds stainless-steel shelving, and I make a guess that it's intended to be a pantry one day, but for now it's empty.

There's a bunker that has a dozen shower stalls and sinks, but everything is missing its hardware. Another is a large kitchen, though no appliances are installed. Just counters and a few coolers. Inside are bags of melted ice, a few cans of soda, and beers.

"How long were they working on this?" Boone asks.

I shrug. "A decade? But it doesn't seem like they got much done. They must have been working construction jobs more than I thought."

"There would need to be some massive generators to power this place," Boone says. "Not to mention if this was built to withstand whatever doomsday scenario Jeremiah feared, it wouldn't work for long unless there were some massive upgrades here."

"It certainly wasn't ready for people to move into. So where would he have taken them?" It feels like we have more questions than answers, though one thing is clear—Jeremiah talked a big talk. But the reality is, Garden Temple is not the flourishing congregation Jeremiah wanted his believers to think it was.

We get farther into the bunkers past several more that are completely empty, and then there's one that seems different. There's a desk, shelving, and a few battery-operated lanterns hanging from the rafters

"Do think it's Jeremiah's office?" Boone asks.

"It would make sense," I say, "that he would have something down here if this is where he spent time when he wasn't at the compound. Most of the time he was at home. That's why, for Lydia, Naomi, and I, our lives were a lot more stifling than some of the other women's. Our husband was always around. He was either at the church, in his office behind the church, or in his bedroom. But I suppose he would have come down here sometimes."

"Did he seem like a hard worker? Like he would have been doing the labor?"

I shake my head. "No, Jeremiah didn't have callouses on his hands, sweat on his clothes. He didn't do the dirty work."

"Sounds like a real leader," Boone says wryly as we step into the office. There's a desk, a few chairs, and filing cabinets. I flip on a lantern, the room awash in the fluorescent glow. There's a bookcase filled with red leather Bibles. On his desk, there is a typewriter, and a manuscript titled *JEREMIAH PRIEST'S ACCOUNT OF THE FINAL DAYS AS GIVEN BY THE DIVINE HAND OF GOD*. His prophecy.

"Have you seen this before?" Boone asks, lifting it up and flipping through it.

"No," I say. "Looks like he was writing his own sacred texts."

"Looks like it. An addendum to the Bible."

"He was inspired by something."

"Drugs?" Boone asks.

"I don't think he did drugs, but I feel stupid saying anything that he didn't do because what do I really know about this man that I was married to for fifteen years?"

"Not married," Boone says.

"Is that clarification important to you?" I ask.

"Kind of," he says. "You weren't legally married to him. So I don't like the idea of you thinking you were."

"I was bound to him, then," I say. "Whether you like it or not, my story is forever linked with his. If he does something terrible to this congregation, I will forever be the wife he took when she was only fourteen. They'll make some documentary about us. Someone will write a story for *The New York Times*, an exposé about the crazy cult in Eastern Washington that finally went to paradise. They'll want to interview me. They'll want to know my side of the story."

"Hey," Boone says, "don't."

"What?" I say, throwing up my arms. "That's what will happen."

"Don't write the ending to your story, Gray."

"I'm just making a point. Sure, I wasn't technically married to the man, but it doesn't change much. I'm still the lady who *married* a maniac, who had three children with him, who couldn't stop him before it was too late."

"Not true," Boone says. "We are going to stop him before it's too late. And we don't even know his plan, Gray."

"How are we going to find him?" I ask. "We're twelve shipping containers deep in his lies, and yet we're no closer to Jeremiah than we were before we left. I have no idea where he is."

Boone shakes his head. "I hate that you're thinking of yourself this way. Like the victim. You're not the catalyst here. You're strong, Gray."

I lift a hand. "That's not for you to say, Boone. I *have* been a victim most of my life, but when I left this place, I was taking a stand. I'm not letting that be my story, okay? Don't tell me what my story can or cannot be."

"I'm not telling you anything," he says. "I just don't want you to live the rest of your life believing lies."

I pick up the manuscript on Jeremiah's desk. "These are the lies."

"You're right," Boone says, "and I think Charlie might like to see this."

"Why would Charlie care?"

"Because she cares about you. She cares about this situation."

"Fine," I say, "take it. Take anything down here you want. Add more reasons for people to judge me."

"Nobody's judging you," Boone says, frustrated now. He grabs a cardboard box and begins filling it with Jeremiah's things. The manuscript, Bibles, a file folder. He reaches for the picture on Jeremiah's table, then he turns it to me. "This you and your sister wives?" he asks.

"Yes," I say. "That's me and Lydia and Naomi." I walk closer, taking the picture from Boone's hands. "Naomi," I repeat, my finger tracing her face.

"What about her?" he asks.

"I just remembered something. When I was talking to Lydia when we couldn't find Ruthie, she told me that Naomi had gone to her sister's."

"When?" Boone asks.

"Just recently, her sister was giving birth and needed Naomi's help and, oh my God ..."

"What is it?" Boone asks.

"Maybe she's still there; maybe she never came back."

"Do you know who the sister is or where she might live?"

"I know her name," I say. "Tracy Charmile. She lives in Spokane. Tracy is Naomi's half sister. They didn't grow up together, but Naomi went to visit sometimes. Tracy's parents divorced when she was young; that's why her mother ended up here at Garden Temple. She was desperate for help, and Jeremiah sure gave it to her, gave it to her in the form of marrying her daughter."

"So you think Tracy is still in Spokane?"

"That's where Naomi was from."

"Do you have a number? Any way we could reach them?"

I shake my head. "No. I don't have any contact information."

"Just a name?"

"Yes."

"Well, I can work with that," he says.

I smile. "Right, you're a detective. You have connections."

"Charlie can get me something."

"Good," I say.

Boone lifts the box.

"Are you really taking all that stuff?" I ask. Boone nods, ready to go. I swallow. "Okay. Well, I'm glad we came down here, then."

"See?" Boone says. "You are a good detective. We hoped something might spark your memory and it did."

We walk out of the underground bunker, weaving our way through this empty, murky place. Outside, the sky is still blue; the day is still young, and I have hope that maybe Naomi is still in Spokane.

Maybe she'll know where our husband went.

18

Once we're back in Boone's car, he cranks up the heat and turns on the seat warmers.

"Thanks, I didn't realize how cold I was," I say, shivering.

With his phone connected to the Bluetooth in his car, Boone dials up Charlie. We're hoping she can help us connect with Naomi's half sister.

"Hey," she says, "everything okay? I've been wondering how you guys are doing out there."

"We're all right," Boone says. "I have Gray here with me now."

"Hi, Gray," Charlie says. "God, you've had one hell of a week."

"You're telling me," I say, appreciating her understanding.

"So what's up? How can I help you guys?" she asks.

"We have a name, Tracy Charmile, but we don't have a phone or a location. I was hoping maybe you might be able to help me out?"

"I can try," she says. "I'm actually at my desk, so this is good timing."

"Awesome," Boone says.

"You guys sure you're okay out there? You don't need any backup?"

Boone tells her how we went to the Grant County Sheriff's Office pleading our case and how Martindale refused to help.

"That's a disappointment," Charlie says, "but I'm not going to say I'm surprised. It's sometimes hard to get bureaucracy on your side even in a big city, and in a small place like that, they trust their own more than they trust outsiders."

"I'm not an outsider," I say. "I lived here for so many years."

"Sure," Charlie says, "but considering what you're asking for, in light of last week, I'm still not surprised."

I frown, hating that she's right.

"But, good news," she says, "I got an address, but there's no number. It's harder these days with cell phones," she says. "I could dig deeper though. I know a guy over in tech who might be willing to help me out."

"That's okay," Boone says. "If we have an address, that's a start. Is it in Spokane?"

"Just outside, in Cheney. It's a college town."

"Thanks," I say, grateful for her quick help.

"Boone, I'll text it to you, and if you guys need more help, honestly, just give me a call. I could be there in five or six hours."

"You'd really do that?" I ask.

"To be honest, when we met, I got pretty intrigued about your life story, Gray."

"I thought that was the case," I say. "You and that tablet of yours. I thought you were writing down notes on me the entire time."

"Not just on you. I kept reading articles about these sects, small groups that have cropped up around the state over the last decade. There's more of them than you'd think."

"It's scary," I say, "to imagine more groups like Garden Temple, that more people have fallen prey to a leader who doesn't actually have their best interests at heart."

"I know," Charlie says, "it *is* scary, but that's

why what you're doing right now is really important. Not just to help your son, but to help all those other people who might get hurt."

"I hope not," Boone says. "I hope we'll get there before anything happens."

We end the call, and Boone plugs the address into the GPS. "It'll be about three hours. You ready to go?" he asks.

I nod. "There's no good coffee in this town, but maybe there's a Starbucks on the way."

Boone grins. "Perfect. So are we listening to classical music or more talk radio?"

"Wow, you're letting me choose?" I appreciate the moment of normalcy. I need it so I don't get swept away by my emotions.

Boone shrugs, turning back onto the highway. "Yeah, you choose."

———

BY THE TIME we get to the address that Tracy is listed at, it's just after two in the afternoon, but I can't think about food right now. I'm more interested in finding my son. And finding Naomi might be a step in the right direction.

Tracy's house is a double-wide on a large

piece of property. I knew from stories Naomi had told how she'd grown up dirt poor and desperate. The broken-down cars in the driveway, the toys and bikes on their sides, and a banged-up front door tell the same story.

"I'm nervous," I admit.

"Go with your gut," Boone says. Isn't that what you're trying to do anyway?"

I nod.

"What's your gut telling you?" he asks.

"That Tracy might know something."

"Good. Then let's go ask her if she does."

When we get to the porch, I hear a baby crying. A newborn. After living with so many little ones for so long at the compound, I can pick up ages of children based on their shouts and shrieks. I can tell the difference between *I'm hungry* and *I'm wet*. This one sounds hungry.

"Who is it?" a woman calls.

"It's Grace, Naomi's sister wife," I say, hoping that gets her attention.

The door pulls open and a woman who looks very much like Naomi looks us over. She has long black hair in a braid to her waist, green eyes so bright they could rival blades of grass. Thick eyebrows and a button nose. She could be a model, she's so beautiful, and she would fit in anywhere if you didn't take into account the clothes she wears, which consist of a dress to her ankles, an apron tied on tight, calico, dingy. Her feet are bare.

"You know where Naomi is?" the woman asks. There's a baby in her arms and a diapered toddler hanging on to her calf.

"No," I say, "I don't. I thought she might be here."

She looks at Boone, then at me. "You're Grace?"

I nod. "Yes. And you're Tracy?"

She nods back. "And who are you?" she asks Boone.

"I'm Orion," he says, offering to shake her hand.

She waves it away and pulls the door open farther to let us in, a baby crying loudly in the background. Inside her home, there are toys everywhere. Cereal and Goldfish in cups on a coffee table with board books, and a cartoon on the television.

"These are mine," she says. "Joseph, Mary, and Elizabeth. This one," she says, pointing to the baby in her arms, "is Lily. I just had her. Isn't she perfect?"

I look down at her newborn. Thick dark

hair, her eyes closed, long lashes just like her mother. "She's beautiful," I say.

"Do you want to hold her?" she asks, thrusting her baby into my arms. "I got to deal with this one." She points to a baby in a bassinet, the baby who's crying loudly.

I rock Lily, looking over at Boone, wondering what he thinks about this situation. It looks like Tracy is the only adult here.

"So you told us the names of your kids," Boone says politely, "but who's that?"

"This is Virtue, Naomi's baby. She's only a few months old."

"Her baby is here? But what about Naomi's other children?" I ask, thinking of Naomi's three older ones.

"Oh, she took them with her."

"Took them where?" I ask.

The woman rolls her eyes, bouncing Virtue on her shoulder. "I need to get her a bottle. She's so fussy."

We follow her into the kitchen. "Do you guys want some tea?" she asks, already putting on a kettle and reaching for a box of tea bags. "I get these down at the co-op. It's a dandelion lemon-balm blend. Heavenly."

I can tell she's sewn her own clothes and her children's clothes. On the stove, there is lentil soup simmering, and a bread maker is on. The whole house smells of sourdough. She would have fit in at the compound perfectly, yet she never came.

"Do you live here alone?" I ask.

She shakes her head. "I live with my husband, Tony; he works in Spokane. He's a plumber. It's good money, which is a good thing considering all these kids we have. Four under four," she says with a smile. "Though it's a blessing, and I wouldn't want it any other way."

"So tell me about Virtue," I say as she pops a silicone nipple in the baby's mouth.

"Well, she's a sweetheart, who loves to fuss." She laughs softly. "Teasing aside, she is a gift from God. Which I know you know all about, Grace." She smiles down at Virtue, who is happily sucking down her bottle. "Naomi came to help me with the birth. She knows what she's doing, now that she's had her fair share, which is a surprise considering how young she is. But she was like you, started early," Tracy says with a shrug, not passing any judgment. The kettle whistles, and she pours three mugs of hot water, handing them out with tea bags. We walk into the living room, but it's so loud that Tracy quickly pivots. "The kitchen table might be a bit quieter. Will you guys settle down?" she calls out to the kids. "I have company."

"Yes, Mama," they say in a chorus.

I smile. "They're well-behaved."

"Considering I just had a baby, they have been adjusting pretty well, and the new TV helps. I'm very thankful Tony finally agreed to get us one. It's long days."

"How long are you watching Virtue?" I ask, wrapping my hands around the steaming mug of tea.

"Till Naomi shows up, which was the plan. Jeremiah gave her permission to go wherever she went. I know you love that man this way and that, but my goodness, he's a control freak."

"Naomi didn't tell you I left the family?"

"She told me you left, but that it was temporary. Was that wrong?" She looks at Boone, then me. "Are you two ..."

I smile at Boone, reminded of how grateful I am that he is here. "Boone is helping me look for my son."

"Your son?" she asks, "I thought you were looking for Naomi."

"I'm looking for them both, I think."

"Well, Naomi came and assisted me with

the birth. She did great. I had another lady from church over helping and the baby popped out in three hours, can you believe it?"

"I can't," I say, indulging her.

"Well, after Lily was born, we had a week where I did a lot of sleeping, and Naomi did a lot of cleaning, and she never complained. But she was getting a lot of phone calls from her husband. Now, Jeremiah doesn't let her have a phone, which I understand. You know, he's got to keep his wife in line. Not everyone believes in the same doctrines, and I don't believe in everything you guys do down there at Garden Temple, but there are a few things that I agree with. And one of them happens to be a woman's place is in her home. You don't really need a phone at your house, do you? I don't have one here."

Boone lifts an eyebrow. "You don't have a telephone?"

"No, why would I need one? I don't have a car either. I mean, you could tell that from out front. Though I suppose if I got a bee in my bonnet, I could try and fix one of those old trucks in the driveway. You probably thought you were driving up to the poor house when you showed up here, but we're not. We're doing just fine. Tony's making good money. And when you pulled in, did you see the foundation we poured? We have four acres. All ours. We're gonna build ourselves a home for our kids. I'm not going back to where I came from."

"And where's that?" Boone asks, his detective hat on.

"I came from a rough neighborhood full of drugs and addicts. I don't want that for my children. God has more in store for us than that."

"I'm happy for you," I say. "And this little bundle of joy is sure perfect," I say, looking down at the baby in my arms. I'm not ashamed to admit there's a twinge of jealousy. There's just something that happens when I hold a newborn in my arms that makes the world feel a little bit better, makes things feel possible.

"So after a week or so," Tracy continues, "Naomi was getting all these calls from Jeremiah. He wanted her home. Well, he could only call when my husband was home at night, and Tony was getting mad because he did not want his phone tied up by Naomi and Jeremiah. He wanted peace and quiet. This is his home, his sanctuary. I know it's a little wild right now, but the little ones are wound up. It's almost nap time."

"Right," I say. "So what did Tony do?"

"Well, Tony called Jeremiah himself. He

asked, 'What's going on with you and your wife that you need Naomi to come home already?' See, we had planned on her staying for a month. Naomi had a car, so she could just take herself home if she needed to. She had enough gas money too. Jeremiah gave her that. He was good to her."

"Right," I say, trying not to laugh, "so good to her."

Tracy doesn't catch on; she's distracted by one of her toddlers who is climbing on the sofa, reaching for a curtain, hankering to pull it down. "Get down, Joseph. You're going to hurt yourself."

"Sorry, Mama." He grins, grabbing another Goldfish cracker and shoving it into his chubby cheek.

"Well, Jeremiah told Tony that Naomi needed to come home then," Tracy explains. "That it was time, that Eden was ready. I didn't know what that meant, but Naomi did. She packed the car up the next morning and put her kids in their car seats."

"So what happened?" I ask. "Why do you have Virtue?"

Tracy lifts an eyebrow. "She didn't want to take Virtue with her. She said Eden was no place for a newborn. That it was underground, and she didn't think the baby would like it."

"So when is Naomi coming back?" I ask.

Tracy looks down at the baby in her arm. "I'm getting the feeling she's not."

19

Tracy's words hang in the air, and I wrap my fingers around the tea mug to steady myself, my mind racing. "Why?"

"What?" Tracy says. "What does Eden even mean? Naomi was being so cryptic, but she'd get like that sometimes. I know how you guys at Garden Temple were. You'd get some new doctrine in your head, or Jeremiah would preach a new message. I remember one year Naomi told me how when you planted your gardens, you could only plant spinach. Apparently any other greens were not holy."

Boone frowns. "What does that even mean?"

Tracy smirks. "I have no idea."

"I remember that," I say. "Jeremiah had

deciphered some text about green gardens growing, and I don't know," I say, shaking my head. "I can't remember the reason behind the spinach. I do remember eating a lot of it that summer though. But this isn't about vegetables, Tracy."

"What do you mean? I thought your men were all building some fancy bunker with hundreds of acres," she said. "The Garden of Eden is paradise, right? Isn't that about big gardens and fruit trees? Where the serpent gave an apple to Eve?"

"Yes, but Jeremiah wasn't talking about a garden when he said Eden. It might have been more metaphorical. He might have been talking about heaven."

"Heaven?" Tracy frowns, bouncing Virtue on her shoulder to burp, the bottle finished and sitting on the kitchen table. "Eden was heaven?"

I nod. "Maybe. And maybe Jeremiah wanted his entire congregation to follow him there."

The room becomes eerily quiet. Even the toddlers who've been bouncing on the couches seem to know something's changed, shifted. They've sat down quietly and are watching their show, completely fixated on the screen.

"You think Naomi did? She took her little ones with her, her toddlers," Tracy whispers. "They're still so young. She ... What do you mean, heaven?" She shakes her head. "I know she was a little out of sorts when she left my house, but Naomi is smart. She's been through a lot. She had those babies back to back. She started when she was fifteen. She's barely twenty now."

Boone looks over at me. Maybe he hadn't realized just how young Naomi was. But I'm young too, barely thirty. I've been in Naomi's shoes.

"Damn it," Boone says. "Sorry for my language. I just, the idea of Naomi going back to him and doing something like that with her kids. I just..." He swallows, looking at Virtue on her aunt's shoulders, eyes now closed, blissfully unaware of the horror that may be happening to the rest of her family.

Tracy's eyes fill with tears. "Grace, tell me I'm missing something. Tell me that this isn't the whole story."

"I don't know what the whole story is," I tell her, explaining everything that I do know. The phone call from Bethany, going to the compound, the religious retreat that wasn't happening at the lodge, the Grant County

Sheriff's Office refusing to help, finding the bunker empty, coming here.

"I'm just glad that when I talked to Lydia last week, she mentioned Naomi coming to stay with you," I say. "Otherwise, I would have never thought of driving up here."

"I'm glad you came," she says. "I just wish" —she kisses Virtue's forehead—"oh, this sweet girl. How could she choose Virtue over her other children?" Tracy shakes her head. "I can't imagine."

I look down at Lily in my arms, glance over at Joseph, Mary, and Elizabeth in the living room. How could you pick between your children?

Then with a horrific sense of shame, I realize I've done that myself. I picked Olive and Ruthie over Abel. When I left Garden Temple, I chose not to tell Abel where I was going. I left him there to his father's devices, and I took my girls and I ran.

I've never felt so disgusting, so twisted in all my life. Children, no matter how old they are, fifteen or five days, they're still innocent. They don't deserve to be picked and chosen like this. I thought I did what I had to do, but did I? Did choosing to leave without Abel lead him down a path that's caused the entire congregation of Garden Temple to blindly follow Jeremiah?

Boone clears his throat. "Tracy, we've got to get going. We've got to find Jeremiah. We've got to find your sister and her kids."

Tracy wipes tears from her eyes. "I wish I could come and help." She looks around her house. "I can't go. Not with all the kids, and Tony's gone."

"It's okay," I say. "You stay here. You have really important work to do looking after these sweet ones." There are tears in my eyes, and I blink them away furiously. "We'll call you."

"You can't call me," she says. "I don't have a phone."

"We'll call Tony, then," I say. "Write his number down, and we'll call as soon as we know something, all right?"

She nods. "Okay. Yes."

"Maybe you should talk to your husband about getting a phone installed here," Boone says. "I'm not trying to overstep, and I understand your convictions, but you're alone on a large piece of property with a lot of children. A phone would be good in case something happened, in case you needed an emergency vehicle, an ambulance, something like that."

Boone's voice is gentle and comforting. "Think about it, okay?"

Tracy nods. "I will."

Lily is sleeping in my arms, and I walk over to the bassinet, placing her there. "I know I'm just Naomi's sister wife," I tell Tracy at the door, "but Virtue is my children's half-sibling. Can I just hold her for a moment?" I ask. "I've never gotten to meet her."

"Oh, Grace, of course." She hands me Virtue, and I decide to walk back through the kitchen with the baby in my arms, needing a moment alone with her, trying to imprint on her heart the love I have for her. "I love you, sweet one," I whisper. "I'll do my best to find your mama. I'll find your brothers and sisters. And no matter what happens," I say, my tears falling freely, "I will always fight for you, however I can. I promise."

I kiss her again, breathing in her perfect baby smell, and I know this double-wide isn't some luxurious house, but this baby doesn't need that. There's warm soup on the stove and bread baking. She has her auntie who loves her, who's a good mom, who's taking care of her kids the best way that she can. Tracy's life may be clouded with a belief system that's forced her to live on the fringes of society, but I don't judge her for that. They're safe. Her children are warm and fed.

And maybe I'm wrong about Tony, but Tracy isn't scared of him, which makes me believe that her children aren't scared of their father.

At the door, I hand Virtue over to her aunt. "Thank you for that," I say, wiping my eyes.

"I gave Orion Tony's number. And I think you're right, Orion. My husband would want me to have a phone here. I don't think we really thought about it like that. Our pastor just told us, you know, that a woman should submit to her husband. And I don't think that necessarily means a woman shouldn't be safe. I don't think Tony would think that either."

Her words give me the peace. I need to get back into Boone's car and leave her there. Once we're on the road, I let out a long breath. "I think she'll be okay. Don't you?"

He nods. And I'm not sure either of us knows who we're talking about, if it's Tracy or Virtue, but maybe it doesn't matter."

As we pull back onto the highway, Boone puts on the classical music, turning the volume up higher than is probably healthy. Tears fill my eyes as the music sweeps over me. Naomi chose to leave Virtue behind. She knew what was coming. She knew what her husband was asking of her. Naomi leaving Virtue behind most likely means death. I look over at Boone. His eyes are filled with tears too.

He looks over, his gaze on mine. "We'll find them, Gray."

If it's not too late.

20

"WE ARE OUT OF TIME; we both know that. Everything Tracy said confirmed my worst fears.

"They're going to kill themselves, Boone," I say. "Where could they be?"

"We gotta think this through, Gray," Boone says, his eyes on the road. "Jeremiah's vindictive, which means he wants you to suffer. You left him. You took his girls from him. He wants you to pay."

"Are you sure?" I ask.

"Your leaving Garden Temple gave him a chip on his shoulder a bit more than I think you're letting yourself believe," Boone says. "He's mad. I saw him at your house a few days ago. Ruthie being kidnapped put your story out there and that pissed him off. He knows he's played all his cards and that time is up. And if he has to go down, he's taking you down with him."

"Me? What would he be trying to do to me besides lure Abel back? Isn't that enough?"

"I'm not sure," Boone says, "but we need to find out. Let's stop somewhere and try to piece things together, okay?"

We drive on the freeway, looking for a place to stop. With the classical music on, we're both lost in our thoughts. When it begins to rain, Boone flips on the windshield wipers and looks over at me.

Tears keep filling my eyes. I'm desperate to drive in a direction that guarantees we will find my son and all the members of Garden Temple. The sky is gray and cloudy, the rain pouring down, the music loud—it feels like we are in a cocoon.

"Should we talk about last night?" he asks finally.

I swallow, biting my bottom lip. "Didn't realize you were such a good dancer. Didn't even need a beat."

Boone laughs softly. "We found a rhythm though, didn't we?" He reaches over and takes my hand. Squeezing it.

"Yeah," I say, wiping the tears from my eyes, thankful for the conversation, a way to distract myself from everything else. "We did."

"There's a Denny's," Boone says, pointing to the next exit. Once we pull off, we head into the diner. I carry in the box of items that Boone took from Jeremiah's office in the underground bunker, along with everything from his safe, and we carry it into the diner to look through.

"How can I help you?" the waitress asks.

"Just coffee, please," Boone says, and I nod in agreement. We slide into a booth and begin sorting through the papers. Most of it is nonsense: Jeremiah's notes that he was making for sermons, chicken scratch, really, talking about the second coming, the harvest, how they're going to drink from the land of milk and honey.

"Do you see anything?" Boone asks as the waitress comes and refills our coffee for the second time.

"Nothing of note." I reach for a Bible and flip through it. I pull out a stack of papers that are tucked between the Psalms.

"What's that?" Boone asks, looking up.

"Uh," I groan with disgust, "it's a photo of Jeremiah and Micah."

"Who's Micah?" Boone asks, taking a drink of coffee.

I press my lips together, trying to think of how to describe him. There are so many things to say about him. "Bishop Micah is Jeremiah's right-hand man, his best friend."

"I have a feeling there is a whole lot more you're not telling me."

"Am I so bad at masking my emotions?"

Boone smiles softly. "Gray, you wear your heart on your sleeve."

"Is that a bad thing?"

He shakes his head. "No. It's a beautiful thing."

Wanting to be honest with Boone, I take a deep breath and explain. "A long time ago, after Abel was born, Jeremiah wanted Micah to be his most trusted confidant. He needed Micah to know how seriously he took their friendship so that they could trust one another, always. He gave Micah a gift. An *offering* is what he called it."

"What was the offering?"

I twirl a spoon in the mug of coffee. "Me."

"You?"

I nod slowly. "Jeremiah said I was the most precious thing he owned, and that sharing me with Micah would prove his commitment."

Boone's jaw clenches, his eyes turning a darker shade of green. "Damn, Gray. Did this happen more than once?"

I shake my head. "No. Turns out Jeremiah realized he was a lot more jealous than he wanted anyone to know. It was a secret one-time thing. Jeremiah had Micah marry a woman named Sarah a few months later. Eventually he took Delilah as well."

"Why did Jeremiah need Micah's confidence so badly?"

"Good question." I lift my shoulders, then let them fall. "But I don't have an answer."

"Was he ... did he ... Micah, did he hurt you?"

I scoff. "I didn't know what pain meant back then. I was a devoted wife, a starry-eyed teenager who would do whatever my prophet asked."

"When did it change? When did you realize not all that glitters is gold?"

"After I lost Esther. I had her eight months after I slept with Micah. She died after two days. I should have been at a hospital, should have had her ..." I stop talking, my emotions overwhelming me. "I'm sorry. I never talk about this. Ever."

Boone reaches out, takes my hand. "I'm sorry, Gray. I'm so sorry."

I lift my eyes, comforted by his touch. "I don't know how you do it," I say. "I had Esther for two days and felt like the world would never be the same. You had Suzannah for years ... then lost her ... I don't know how you do it."

"Grief isn't like stitches after surgery; it doesn't just heal over time," Boone says. "It's with you forever. A part of you. My grief in losing Suzy? It's never going away."

"I'm sorry you understand this pain so well."

"Life isn't easy, is it?" Boone sighs. "Do you know if Esther was Jeremiah's or—"

I cut him off. "I have no idea, and honestly, it doesn't matter. It was a long time ago. And then I had Olive and Ruthie—healthy, happy girls. I can't ask for more." When the waitress comes over and refills our coffees I thank her before opening up more to Boone. "Micah didn't hurt me, not like you'd think. He thought he was God's gift to women; you'd probably call him a playboy. Jeremiah was stern, a force to be reckoned with, but Micah was all smiles, flirtatious, and funny. The opposite of his prophet."

"What did he do at the compound?" Boone asks.

"He was the worship leader," I say, reaching back for the Bible. I laugh, shaking my head. "That guy was a real piece of work. If Jeremiah wasn't so sure of himself, Micah would be the one running the show."

"Anything else in that book?" Boone asks, pointing to the Bible in my hands.

"It looks like more deeds," I say.

"The properties that people handed over to Jeremiah when they joined the church?"

"I think so, except ..." I frown. I pause, staring at the paper in my hand, shaking my head in confusion. "This one is my parents' farm in Wenatchee, 611 Cherry Blossom Lane."

"The family farm that you had as a kid?"

I nod. "Yeah, and when I moved into Garden Temple, my aunt and uncle told me according to my parent's will, they had to sell the farm to pay off my parents' debts. If they did that, Jeremiah wouldn't have the deed, which means they were lying," I say, looking at the paper in my hands, feeling a swell of emotions connecting me to the past, a time in my life that was pure joy, happiness, bliss. My childhood.

"What are you thinking?" Boone asks.

"I'm thinking Genevieve reminded me how vindictive Jeremiah really is. And Tracy was certain everyone went to Eden—a place not fit for a newborn... Maybe ..."

"What?" Boone asks.

I twist my lip, hating the thought. I shake my head. "No, it can't be."

"It can't be what? Say what you're thinking. I can't read your mind."

"I'm thinking maybe Jeremiah went there. Maybe they're at the farm. This could be Jeremiah's way of being vindictive. What better way to make me pay than bringing the people I love to my family farm and killing them."

Boone nods, catching on. "Turning the one place you hold dear into a burial ground, taking your memories of good times and ruining them."

"If that's true, and he's really doing that, we have to go," I say, blinking back tears wrought with fear. "Now. Wenatchee's two hours' drive."

"You really think he would do that?" Boone asks.

I shake my head. "After everything Genevieve and Tracy said, yes. I should've thought of it before."

"You thought the property was gone, sold."

"Of course Jeremiah would do something like this," I say. "We need to go. Now."

Boone nods, calling the waitress over as I

begin putting the papers and files back in the box. "Can we get a few sandwiches to go?"

As he walks over to the register to pay for the food, I pack everything up. As I load the box, a photograph falls to the table.

I pick it up, my heart sinking. It's a picture of me at ten years old with my aunt and uncle and Jeremiah. His arm is around me, as if I were his property even then. We were at a lake, and I remember that day so distinctly. It was the day Jeremiah baptized me.

I had only been at the compound for a few months, but my salvation was at stake, they'd all told me. I needed to make a promise, a covenant to secure my place in the garden.

I didn't understand all of it, but I'd wanted so desperately to feel safe. I had been missing my parents terribly, and I wanted to feel connected to something. Someone.

A garden of eternal life? A family that would never leave me? Even in death we'd be together? I needed to believe in those magical promises that Jeremiah offered.

Looking at the picture with new eyes, I see myself as a little girl desperate to believe in the impossible.

Now, I'm a grown woman and feel just as desperate.

I need to believe my son is still alive, even if everything is telling me that it's too late.

I tuck the photograph into my purse. Not because I want to remember my baptism, not because I want to remember my aunt and my uncle or Jeremiah, but because I want to remember that little girl who held on to hope.

I need that hope right now. Today.

I will find my son. Because if this little girl could hold on to hope, so can I.

21

IN THE CAR, Boone pulls up directions to the farm in Wenatchee. "It's closer than you thought. It's only ninety minutes away."

As Boone begins the drive to Wenatchee, I try to calm my mind, but I'm restless, anxious. My fingers tap the console, and my feet jump up and down. I'm not usually an anxious person, not like this. I'm pretty good at holding my emotions in, except for the tears, of course. I'm an unabashed crier, but surprisingly, there are no tears right now. I'm full of nervous energy, hope mixed with a prayer.

"Calm down," Boone says. "You're making me nervous."

"I can't help it," I say. "What if we're too late?"

"Why don't you eat something?" he says. "That might help the time pass faster."

I reach into the paper sack from the diner and pull out a sandwich.

"Do you mind unwrapping mine for me too?" he asks.

"Of course," I say, pulling back the paper and offering him the roast beef on sourdough.

"Thanks," he says, giving me a quick smile, then keeping his eyes on the road.

I begin eating and reach to flip the radio to something more upbeat than his classical music.

He lifts an eyebrow. "Wow, okay, so you're taking control now, huh?"

"Isn't that what I ought to be doing with my life?" I tease as pop music fills his car. I immediately laugh, though, because the lyrics discuss bumping and grinding, things I have never done in my life and don't plan on doing anytime soon.

"How about we compromise?" he suggests, turning the radio to another station, oldies. "This is classic rock and roll."

"Okay, I can dig it."

Boone laughs. "Dig it, huh? Wow, you really are in a good mood."

"I am. I feel like maybe it's crazy to feel so

hopeful, but I am. I want to believe that Abel's okay. That everyone is okay. Even if I know that I have no reason to feel so optimistic."

"I hope they are too," Boone says. He doesn't say more, that my uncharacteristic optimism might be for nothing. That we might have taken too long to come to this conclusion. That we might have followed another dead end, desperate for a lead.

When we finish eating, I suggest we call Charlie. There's an hour left of the drive, and I want to fill her in on what's been going on.

Boone's phone is connected to the Bluetooth in the car, so I pull up Charlie's number, calling her through the speaker.

"Hey, Boone," she says. "I was hoping you'd call. Where are you guys now?"

"Hey, Charlie," I say. "Boone's driving. I'm in the passenger seat."

"And where are you guys headed?" she asks.

"Wenatchee," I say, and then I get her up to speed with the situation, specifically the deed we've found, the reminder from Genevieve about Jeremiah's vindictive personality and Tracy's account of what led to Naomi leaving without her youngest child, headed to Eden. "So we're hoping he's there to try and get the final say, to take something from me."

Boone snorts. "He's already taken quite a bit."

Even though Charlie isn't in the car with us, I swear I can hear her thinking. "What?" I ask. "I feel like you're not saying something."

"I think you're going to need backup," she says. "If Jeremiah isn't at this farm, then he's still on the loose, and you're right, Gray: time is running out. I want to come."

"Sure," I say. "If you can take time off work, of course I want you with us." Boone looks over at me, nodding in agreement, his eyes dark. He understands the gravity of what we are driving toward. And he wants another cop close by he can rely on.

"Good," Charlie says. "Because I'm already on the highway."

I give Charlie the address we're headed to, and since Wenatchee is about halfway between Tacoma and Spokane, she says she expects to get there the same time we do, and that she'll call when she's close.

When she ends the call, I look over at Boone. "Are you okay?"

"In a word, no. I'm protective of you, Gray. And after last night, it's more than that."

"What do you mean?" I ask, setting the phone in my lap, looking over at Boone as he keeps his eyes on the road. His profile is so handsome. His beard has grown in by now, his reddish-blond hair flecked with gold, freckles on his cheekbones, his eyes as green as a forest.

"You know I care about you," he says, reaching over and squeezing my thigh. Usually a touch like that would cause me to tense, to freeze up, but that's not how I am with Boone. Not anymore. I take his hand and lace my fingers through his.

"You know what I hope for?" I tell him.

"To find your son in one piece?" he asks.

"Yes, that is what I hope for, but I hope for more things too, Boone."

"Like what?" he asks.

"A life that is happy. You know, before I left, Olive told me something. She said when we were talking about you—"

Boone cuts me off. "You were talking about me?"

"Stop it," I say, laughing despite the situation we are in. "The girls were certain that I had a crush on you."

Boone's eyebrows lift. He takes his eyes off the road for a split second and finds mine. "A crush, huh?"

"Yes, a crush," I say. "And they were right, I did have a crush on you, or *something*."

"It's not just something," he says, squeezing my hand. "It's *something real.*"

"Agreed," I say. "But what Olive was saying was that I deserved to have a happy life. I tried to tell her that my life has been full and happy, that being their mother was the honor of my life, but she insisted that there is a difference between being fulfilled as a mother and being fulfilled as a person."

"And what do you think about that?" Boone asks.

"She's right. I mean, for a twelve-year-old, the girl's pretty smart."

"I couldn't agree more," Boone says.

"But it's been so scary to imagine a life beyond running away from Jeremiah. I've been surviving for so long, but then I meet you. I mean, I don't even know where you live. I've never been to your cabin. I've never met your parents. You're a mystery to me in so many ways."

Boone clears his throat. "I'm not a mystery to you in the ways that matter," he says. "What I've told you is the truth. I'm not harboring any secrets. My cabin, sure, you haven't been there, but I can imagine it's not that hard to picture. It's got one bedroom and a kitchen, a recliner, and a TV that's embarrassingly large. It's not a home. It's a place I go to sleep. You know how you said Olive wants you to have a more fulfilling life, not just as a mother, but as a person?"

"Yeah," I say.

"I want that for me too. I want my life to be about more than the work I do for the police department. I want a life with somebody, a family, a future."

The air in the car seems swallowed up. The only sound I hear, even though the music is on, is the pulse of my heartbeat as my fingers entwine with Boone's.

Boone hasn't made me any promises about forever, but when he speaks, I know that what we share isn't temporary. "I still want to see your cabin," I tell him.

He smiles. "Well, I want to show it to you."

We drive in silence for a few minutes before my worry gets the best of me again. "Do you think Abel's going to be okay?" I ask, doubt finding its way back into the conversation.

"Yes, of course he is."

"How can you be so sure?"

Boone exhales, eyes on the road. "You're right, Gray. You know, when Ruthie was missing, I told you that everything would be all right. That she'd come home in one piece."

"And she did," I interject.

"Yeah," Boone said, "but those weren't promises I should have ever made. They weren't guarantees that I could make certain to fulfill."

"But those words were filled with hope, and I needed that."

"I know," he says, "but still, is it fair to make promises when they're not something you can guarantee?"

"I don't know," I say.

"I'm sorry I made those promises about Ruthie. I think after losing Suzanne, the idea of losing another little girl scared the hell out of me. And it wasn't just any little girl, it was your little girl, your baby."

"I'm still glad you made those promises," I say. "Because when you spoke, I knew where you were coming from. You were coming from a place of understanding because you'd been there. You'd lost your most precious thing."

"Then I want to promise you the world, Gray. I want to promise you that your family can be knit back together somehow. Even if I'm not sure how it will happen. I guess holding on to hope is better than nothing." Boone lifts my hand and kisses the back of my palm. "We're almost there," he says.

He's right, Wenatchee isn't far off now. We're close to the family farm that holds my happiest memories.

I close my eyes, praying that the farm on Cherry Blossom Lane hasn't turned into a graveyard.

22

As we pull onto 611 Cherry Blossom Lane, the first thing I notice is the house. "It looks just the same," I whisper.

Boone drives slowly up the long drive as I take in the farmhouse. It's not large, but it's white, though in need of a fresh paint job. Still, it's beautiful. The porch is big and wide. There are rocking chairs across the front, a big farm door that welcomes you into a foyer and a living room. I remember that there's a fireplace and built-in cabinets, and I can see it all as if I'm standing in the house right now.

Memories flood back as I take in the view.

My mom making an apple pie in the kitchen, my dad pulling out an ice cream maker from the basement, filling it with rock salt and ice, heavy whipping cream and a real vanilla bean, which we all marveled at. We had apple pie à la mode on that big front porch, the three of us. I can taste those caramelized apples, the sweet cinnamon, the vanilla ice cream melting in my mouth. My mom's laugh. She had the best laugh. And she was beautiful. Her eyes were clear and her hair was long. Olive resembles her. I see my mother in Olive's coloring and nose and the slant of her eyes. I wish my mom could have met her, met all of my children.

"You okay?" Boone asks, squeezing my hand.

"I'm okay. It's just a lot, being back here."

As we reach the top of the drive, I gasp at what's before me, realizing I'm not okay at all. The sweet memories fade as I take in the rows of cars, dozens of them, trucks and vans. There is nothing identifying them as cars of the members of Garden Temple, but I know it's them. I know they're here.

Jeremiah's safe led us to this place, and maybe he never thought we would show up, figure out the clues, and drive here.

But he was planning on ruining this place for me, whether I knew it or not.

I won't let him. He's already taken enough. I won't let him take this too.

Boone puts the car in park near the back door of the farmhouse. I jump out before he's even turned off the engine. "Gray, let's think this through."

I shake my head. "There's no more time for thinking. There's only time for doing. Boone, I have to go get my son." I run from the car and pull open the back door of the farmhouse, calling for Abel.

He doesn't answer. No one does.

The house is empty. I don't know what I was expecting. If they were here, they'd be spilling into the yard.

I race through the rooms quickly, feeling like I'm back at the compound going through the houses, looking for someone, anyone. There's nothing. No one dead or alive.

Boone is in the kitchen when I finish racing through the house. "Maybe they're in the barn," he says. "Come on." He grabs me by the wrist. "Gray. You need to stay calm. Okay? Jeremiah is a dangerous man. We can't let him hurt you."

I swallow, heeding Boone's words, knowing his advice is sound. He's served his entire life as a police officer. He knows how to apprehend a bad guy, how to take down someone who's dangerous. "This is your fight," he says. "I'm not trying to get in the way of that. I just want to make sure at the end of it, you're all right."

I nod, knowing he's right. I can't get careless now.

We walk toward the barn, hearing music coming from inside, voices singing. "How Great Thou Art" ringing out. I hear Bishop Micah inside, his voice loud and clear, leading the congregation in song and prayer.

We move faster, jogging toward the sound, but before we even get to the big doors of the old red barn, we're greeted by a man I know so very well.

Jeremiah has stepped out of the big, red barn doors, hands on his hips, like he has been waiting for us.

My jaw tightens; my back straightens; my eyes pierce his.

"Where is he?" I ask Jeremiah. "Where is Abel? You lured him out here. You made him come. If something has happened to him, I swear, Jeremiah, I will never forgive you."

"Grace. What kind of hello is that for your husband? For the father of your children?" He looks over at Boone, smirking. "What kind of greeting is that for the prophet who's going to take you to paradise?

"I'm not going anywhere with you," I say, my anger rising with each syllable.

"Of course you will. Now, where are my daughters?" he asks, looking behind me at Boone, giving him a scathing look. I'm not surprised—Boone is a direct threat to his sense of power.

"You think I would bring them here?"

Jeremiah changes his tactic. "I was hoping you'd put it all together. You didn't think I would sell this place that's so precious to you. Did you?"

"My aunt and uncle told me they sold it to pay my parents' debts." I shake my head, trying to read Jeremiah's body language, but he's as impenetrable as ever.

"They gave me the deed," Jeremiah says. "I told them I was going to take care of everything and I did. I knew this place was special. Special to you. So I wouldn't let anything happen to it, Grace. Not to you, my first wife."

"Stop it," I say. "We're not going down memory lane. I just need Abel."

Jeremiah unclips a walkie-talkie from his belt. "Do you want me to call him? He's inside the barn right now with the rest of the congregation. We've all been waiting for a sign from our Heavenly Father. And Grace, that sign is you."

"What do you mean, waiting?"

"Waiting, praying, asking God to deliver us, and look—you heard our prayer. You came. Everyone will be so pleased that you're joining us."

"I'm not joining you. I'm not going anywhere with you."

"So you want to watch as we all enter the garden? Will you be able to live with yourself, Grace, knowing you didn't join us?"

"Stop it," I say, raising my hands in frustration. Wanting Abel here, wanting Jeremiah's madness to end.

Boone steps forward, Jeremiah shakes his head. "Why did you bring him?" Jeremiah asks. "He doesn't understand us, our work here."

"Our work here? Why don't you tell me what *your* work is?" I ask. "I went to the bunker, you know. Why didn't you just take everybody down there to carry out this twisted plan of yours?" I ask him. "Why here? Why this place?"

"You know why, Grace. This is for you." He grins widely, a smile that made my heart flutter when I was a teenage girl and now makes me sick inside.

"Just give me my son," I say. "And let your wives out. Think of all of those people inside that barn. There are children in there, Jeremiah. You can be better than this. I know you can."

Jeremiah lifts his walkie-talkie and speaks. "Abel, I need you out here." Then he scoffs. "You're going to like this. You think our boy is yours, but he's not. He was always mine, and he's going with me to the end."

"No," I shout as Abel steps from the side door of the barn, walking toward his father, his eyes not meeting mine. "Why won't everyone in there just come out?" I ask. "Come out and put a stop to this!"

Jeremiah shakes his head. "Grace. They don't want this to stop. This is what they've devoted their entire lives to; this is our purpose. We're going to Eden together. Today. Your arrival has sealed our fate."

"It doesn't have to be this way," I plead, but even as I say it, I know how flat the words are, how false. It does have to be this way because Jeremiah knows there is no coming out of this without spending the rest of his life in prison.

Boone, though, is about to make a move. I sense it. He is here to help, and I watch his hand move to his pocket, reaching for his gun.

Jeremiah shouts, "Don't you dare!" He grunts, pulling out a gun from inside his jacket pocket.

I tense. Boone does too.

He knows what he's done—done to all the people here. He's convinced them to hand over their assets, their entire lives. He's evaded federal income taxes for decades, and worse than that, he married the children of his followers. He's a rapist and a pedophile. And that is just what I know. What other secrets does he have hidden?

He knows he's in a corner, a corner I've put him in. Part of me feels like this is all my fault, but that's ridiculous. I know that now. I'm strong enough now to separate my part in all of this from his.

"Abel," I say. "Don't listen to him. Come with me. Come on, honey. You can just come, get in Boone's car right now, and we can go back home."

"Home?" Abel asks, frowning. "What does home mean to you, Mom?"

I swallow, scared. Seeing my son as I remember him from before I left the compound with the girls, knowing he was his father's child, not mine. Not trusting that if I told him what I was doing, planning on running away, he would keep my secret.

I was scared he would go straight to his dad and tell him my plans.

Maybe it was intuition that told me to go without him, because as I stand here now, his shoulder lined up with his father's, it's impossible to imagine him being on my side.

Boone steps behind me, using the argument I'm having with Jeremiah to make a move. He rushes toward the door where Abel exited.

"Where do you think you're going?" Jeremiah shouts.

"I'm going in there to help these people," Boone says, a fire in his eyes.

"No, you're not," Jeremiah hollers. "Stop."

Boone doesn't listen. "Gray," he calls out to me. "Get your son. Get in the car. Call nine-one-one."

Jeremiah, though, doesn't like the sound of that. Not at all.

As Boone reaches the door of the barn, Jeremiah raises his gun to Boone, a shot knocking him sideways. He drops to his knees, groaning in agony.

Blood seeps through the fabric of his flannel shirt as he clutches himself.

I stumble toward him, screaming as he falls to the ground, the shot ringing in my ears.

No. Not Boone.

23

"BOONE," I cry. The bullet has hit him straight in the chest, and blood saturates his flannel shirt.

He's holding his hand against his wound as blood seeps through his fingers. I'm scared, scared that it's all too late. That it's all over before it began.

Abel looks at me like I'm a stranger as Boone bleeds out on the ground. I drop to the grass, ripping off my sweater, pressing it to his wound. "Help them," Boone grunts. "The children inside."

The barn is full of people who are my family, my sister wives, my friends. And I know he is right. I want to sit here, soothing him, but there is no time.

I stand, running toward Jeremiah, wanting to shove him to the ground, take his gun, and hold him hostage for a change.

Jeremiah turns, pointing his gun at me. "Don't take another step, Grace. Do exactly as I say."

"Or what?" I ask. "You'll shoot me too?"

Jeremiah's eyes are cold and dark, full of hate. Hate for me. Maybe hate for himself. I don't know. He's narcissistic and delusional. I don't know what Jeremiah thinks anymore, beyond his own invincibility.

He's believed for far too long that he has power over the people who have congregated around him, trusting in him, perpetuating the story he's told himself that he is God; he is their savior, that he will take them to a holy place.

But there is no place that is holier than a home. And these people gave Jeremiah the deeds to their houses when they moved onto the compound. They have nothing left because they gave it all to Jeremiah already. They've had faith in him, a man who's more a monster than a messiah.

"Listen to me, Abel. You don't have to do what your father says. You can come with me," I cry. My eyes are blurry with tears, fear coursing through my veins. I shake. I tremble.

I'm terrified of losing every last thing I love in a desperate plea for freedom, my own freedom, freedom for my girls.

"Abel," I say, "I'm sorry I left you with him. I should have brought you with me."

It's the cry of a mother's heart that I hope my son hears, but Jeremiah just laughs. "He's not going anywhere with you now. He's coming to Eden, with me." Jeremiah has the gun pointed at me, and it forces me to stay in place.

I wish I were closer, that I could reach out and grab it from him, but I can't. Right now, he is in control, and that's where he's always wanted to be.

A commotion distracts him though. The door of the barn opens, and someone steps over Boone, who is lying in front of the door, bleeding out, maybe taking his last breath.

But Boone is not the only one bleeding because out steps Bethany.

Abel's Bethany. And her dress is covered in blood.

"Prophet, I need help," she begs. "Abel," she cries, "help me. I'm losing the baby." She sobs. Her shoulders shake. She looks down at Boone, then looks away as if unable to process what's happening. The fear in her eyes is feral. I feel it to my core. I want to reach out and hold her, give her a hug because her family is inside that barn, and they have not chosen to protect her.

"Abel," she sobs, "our baby."

"*Your* baby?" Jeremiah looks at his son with disgust. "You laid with a woman I was going to spend eternity with?"

"I've always loved her, Dad." Abel's shoulders fall as he takes in his dearest friend, the girl he has loved since he was a child. "Bethy," he says, tears on his cheeks, "it's the stress, I think, of the last few days."

Of course she has been under undue stress. Jeremiah called for them all to take their lives, asked them to leave the compound, come here for the final days.

Bethany, though, is shaken to her core. Her dress is covered in blood, and she collapses to her knees. Her arms wrap around her waist in pain as she loses the baby, the tiny seed of hope, a child created from love.

That's what I want. I look at Boone. Is it what I could have had?

I'll never know because he's dying and Abel's baby is gone and Bethany is broken and Jeremiah still has the gun pointed at my head, and I don't know how I'm supposed to stop this.

How do you stop the workings of a

madman?

I wish there was time to find out.

Abel moves to her side, helping her down to the ground. She clings to him, but he has business to finish. Abel turns on his father, fury in his eyes. "You did this," he shouts. "You did this to her."

"I never slept with her," Jeremiah seethes. "That was your sin, son."

"My sin? No. She's suffering because of you. Because of you, Dad. You did this to her."

Jeremiah shakes his head. "No, look at all the suffering in this world, Abel. This is why we need to go to Eden, to leave this behind. There, you can be with your baby. Bethany will be there too. Of course, you'll have to atone for your sins in heaven as you would have on earth for taking a woman who wasn't your wife. But Abel, there will be forgiveness in Eden. We will go together. We're going to go into the barn, and we'll finally be where we've always dreamt of going."

But Abel looks at Jeremiah with rage that no longer merely simmers at the surface. My son's hands are fists, his body shakes.

Jeremiah looks back at me. "And you, you're not coming even if you beg on your hands and knees. I won't let you. You're not worthy of

Eden. You can't even keep your kids safe." He points to Boone. "And he certainly can't protect you."

Abel shouts, "Mom doesn't need a man to protect her."

Jeremiah seethes. "You don't deserve our family."

Abel shakes his head. "Our family? What does family even mean to you, Dad? Family means taking care of your children." He points at the blood on Bethany's dress. "Your grandchild. Not taking the girl your son loves as your own wife." Abel's fists are clenched. He looks more like a man than a boy. "You're not a prophet, and I won't help you anymore. I trusted you too many times, and you've always let me down. I won't let it happen again."

Jeremiah turns toward his son, gun raised, and I fear he is going to shoot him in cold blood. I can't stand by and let it happen.

Knowing that Abel is truly on my side, I realize this is my chance, my one and only opportunity to take control. Boone points to the gun at his side, and I dive for it, wanting to lean down and hold him tight.

But I don't have time.

I take the gun, and I point it at Jeremiah's back as he shouts at his son.

I may have killed before, but I've never shot someone.

Somehow it feels right. The cold metal in my hands. The weight of the trigger against my finger.

Bethany and Boone are bleeding out, broken. Jeremiah is oblivious to me. His rage is now directed at his son, and I take my chance.

At the last second, he turns to me, knowing it's too late, that my gun is raised, and my finger is on the trigger. And his eyes, they aren't filled with shame—they are written with nothing but hate.

I point and I shoot, without regret.

The shot is different than the one that hit Boone. Maybe it's because the sound is so sweet.

Is that a perverse thought as Jeremiah's blood splatters against Abel's face? Against the red wood of the barn. His brains on the ground, his body falling over headfirst.

I never get a last look in my husband's eyes and I'm glad.

I'm thirty years old and have seen way too much for a woman my age.

Jeremiah dead on the ground is one thing I never saw coming. But my God, it is a glorious sight.

24

JEREMIAH IS facedown on the ground. He's not moving. He never will again. I look up at Abel, and his eyes are not filled with horror; they're filled with nothing but relief.

"Mom?" he whispers. "You saved my life."

I drop to Boone's side, not the man who gave me my children. It's Boone's life that hangs in the balance. I'm on my knees, my tears falling on his cheeks.

"Boone. Don't go. I can't lose you."

"Damn it, Gray," he grunts. "It wasn't supposed to happen like this. I promised you everything would be okay and—"

"Shh," I say, pressing my fingers to his lips, realizing the bullet he took is lower than I thought, on the right side, at his ribs.

"I can't lose you," I tell him. "Not after I just found you."

"Good," he says. "Because I sure as hell am not going anywhere without you."

I kiss him. He's bleeding and breathless and I don't care. I kiss him because Boone means the world to me.

"I love you, Gray," he murmurs. "You know that?"

"I love you too."

The words are not a shock to my system. They are the truth that I've known nearly since the day we met. This is the man I'll never live without.

The door to the barn pulls opens as I grab the phone from Boone's pocket. I press 9-1-1 as the barn doors reveal the entire congregation of Garden Temple.

Hundreds of people start screaming, shouting. The family I lived with for nearly all of my life are horrified at what they see.

Their prophet dead before them. A gun at my side. Bishop Micah is crying out, calling for help, kneeling next to his closest friend. Sister wives and children are shouting, pleading for deliverance.

"Hello?" an operator says. "Can I help you?"

"I'm at 611 Cherry Blossom Lane. I'm here

with two hundred people who have been held captive by Jeremiah Priest. He is dead. I just shot him and we need an ambulance. There's a cop here, bleeding from a bullet wound, and a woman who's suffering a miscarriage. We need help. We need help right now."

"Ma'am, can I keep you on the line? Are you safe?"

I look at the gun next to me, the man dead before me. I hold Boone's hand, squeeze it tight.

"I'm safe." I tell her. "I'm safe now."

I drop the phone, watching as my sister wives, Lydia and Naomi, come out of the barn. The congregation is swarming around them. There's a table in the center of the barn filled with cups, hundreds of paper cups filled with juice, and the terror washes over me.

"How close were you guys to ...?" I ask Abel as he reaches for Jeremiah's gun, taking it for safekeeping.

"Minutes, Mom. Dad was losing it. He said the time was coming. He'd been preaching for twelve hours, maybe more. Everybody was near fainting, delirious. We were thirsty and dehydrated. We knew he had a gun, and we were scared to try and leave, but the only thing to drink was the poison on the table."

Abel cradles Bethany in his arms. She's sobbing against his chest, her body in so much pain. That poor, sweet girl; she's just lost so much. Somehow she knows that I need help too. She hands me her apron, and I press the fabric to Boone's side, hoping it can help stop some of the blood.

My sister wife Lydia falls beside Jeremiah, rolling him over. He's been shot so horrifically that I feel ill as she takes in what is left of his head.

"You did this to him, Grace!" Lydia shouts. "You killed our prophet!" Her finger waves, her anger boils.

Naomi, though, has her children with her —in her arms, clinging to her legs. I think of Virtue with her Aunt Tracy in Spokane. Thank God that child won't suffer from this trauma because the children here right now in this barn are going to suffer from years of PTSD.

I hate Jeremiah, but Lydia, she hates me. "We were supposed to go to Eden together!" She runs into the barn and grabs one of the cups of juice.

"Don't," I cry. "Lydia, you don't have to."

But it's too late, she's taken it, swallowed it. And I watch as a few other people do the same. Martha, Bishop Grove's wife, reaches for a glass and drinks. I'm terrified as Naomi walks toward the table with her children in her arms.

"Don't!" I shout. "Think of Virtue."

"I am," she says as her eyes find mine.

It's like she's finally seeing the light. She reaches the table and kicks it over with her heel.

And damn, I've never been more proud of my sister wife.

Lydia, though, is already clutching her stomach, realizing what she's just done. Martha too. I see a few men who had reached for glasses before the table was knocked over, and they're also experiencing the torture of whatever poison Jeremiah put in those cups.

I hear a siren blare, and I cling to the hope I've been holding on to since I got in the car this afternoon.

Jeremiah is dead, and maybe Lydia is about to be too. But the fact that so many people are still standing is a blessing.

I look at Abel. "I thought I lost you."

He reaches for my free hand. He holds it tight. "Mom," he says, "I've always been with you."

And I realize he has because we've been holding one another in our hearts all this time.

The ambulance pulls up to 611 Cherry

Blossom Lane. The family farm that I thought had been gone for decades is mine. It's here.

A medic runs out; police arrive on the scene, and I exhale.

I killed a man. I look down at Boone, praying that I saved another.

25

I HOLD Boone's hand as he is lifted onto a gurney and brought to the ambulance. Emergency responders have him connected to an IV and are cleaning the wound. Bethany is being loaded into another ambulance, and Abel is right at her side. I want to go with them, but I've just killed a man. The police are detaining me until they decide whether to press charges.

As we get in the backs of our respective emergency vehicles, Abel's eyes meet mine once again.

"I love you, Mom," he says.

"I love you more. I'll see you soon. Okay?"

They're headed to the Wenatchee Hospital. The sirens blare as the ambulance rolls down Cherry Blossom Lane, and I hope next time

Abel and Boone arrive back here, it will be without so many police officers, without so many investigators and reporters. The entire farm is covered with responders.

Above us, helicopters circle for local news coverage, and I know once this story breaks, it will be a national headline.

I always said I didn't want to be interviewed as Jeremiah's wife, assuming I knew how the story would be framed and how I'd look.

But now, as an officer asks me to explain what just transpired, I realize maybe telling my side of the story isn't the worst thing.

Because my story is one of a survivor. And maybe the world needs more stories like that. Stories about women who said enough was enough, who chose to stand up and fight back, fight for the life they wanted, fight for the people they love.

———

"GRAY?"

I turn and see Charlie has arrived at the farmhouse, her car lost in the sea of vehicles. Police officers, social workers, EMTs, reporters. The property is flooded as members of Garden Temple begin to go through what will be hours, maybe days of questioning.

I'm so thankful Charlie's here, to help me navigate this. I just want to get to the hospital, to be with my family.

She steps closer, pulling me into a hug. "Oh, girl." She shakes her head. "Is Boone okay?"

I nod. "I think so," I say, tears in my eyes. "He's on the way to the hospital now. I just—"

"I know," she says, pulling me back in for another hug, and God, it feels good. "And your son?" she asks, squeezing my hand. "Is he okay?"

"I'm guessing you've been listening to the news?" I ask.

"Yeah, I stopped at a gas station to fill up and I checked Twitter, and the next thing I knew, I was seeing all these pictures and videos. And I realized, crap, I was late, too late to help."

"No, if you'd been here, it might've meant one more person got hurt."

"Your son?" she asks again.

I exhale. "He's okay. He's with Bethany right now, headed to the hospital too."

She frowns. "Oh no, is Bethany okay?"

"She lost the baby. I think she was about

ten weeks along. She's taking it hard, as she should. She's still just a child herself."

"It's never easy," Charlie says, and I realize she knows a thing or two about loss. Maybe we all do, every one of us here, not just in Wenatchee, but in the whole wide world.

We're all carrying pieces of our past that have shaped us, made us who we are. Maybe we're not the people we want to be, but the fact we're standing with our lungs full of air, breathing in and out, is a miracle in and of itself.

I'm not the only survivor. All of us are survivors in our own way.

Later, after I am released, Charlie drives me to the hospital.

"Thank you for coming," I say as we round into the parking lot.

"Thank you for letting me."

"I take it you're pretty interested in Jeremiah?"

She shrugs. "Yeah, I've always had a thing for cults."

I smirk. "And you met me, and you thought you hit a goldmine?"

"Not like that, but it just reminded me of how many so-called prophets are out there, holding people captive just like he did. My stepdad lost years of his life to the Brethren in Nevada back in the 90s. I was always intrigued by his stories."

I swallow. "Well, maybe that can be what you do now, take down one cult at a time."

"Yeah, I guess I'll have to keep you on retainer though, to help me with the ins and outs."

I smile. "Hey, anything you need. If there's a way I can help bring some sort of understanding out of all of this mess, I want to do it."

At the hospital, they tell me I have to stay in the waiting room, which kills me because I want to be with Boone every step of the way. God knows he's been with me every step of mine.

But I do as they ask, and when they tell me I should call anyone related to him, I pull out his phone, the one I used to call 9-1-1, and scroll through the numbers. I find his sister and I press dial, swallowing as I try to think of what I'm going to say to this woman I hardly know. But when she picks up, I realize she knows, without my saying anything, that something bad has happened.

"What is it?" she asks. "Orion, what's happened?"

"It's not Orion," I say. "This is Gray West, Boone's friend."

"Oh," she says. "What's going on? Orion never calls. When his number showed up, I assumed the worst."

"It is the worst," I say, "or very nearly." I tell her what happened in simple enough terms. "He's with the doctor now. They're going to operate on him."

"Is it life threatening?"

I swallow. "I don't think so. You know how strong Boone is."

"Yeah, I do. Oh God, this is so shocking," she says.

"I'm sorry to call like this. I just thought you would want to know."

"Oh no, I'm so glad you did. Should I come?"

"How about I call you as soon as I know more? It shouldn't be long. I know it sounds a little callous to say it's just one gunshot, but there was only one bullet and it went through, and he was breathing when I saw him last. His eyes were open. He was alert."

"Thank God," she says, "and thank God you're with him. I know how much he cares about you."

I promise her I'll call back with an update

as soon as I can, and then I place another call, this one more intimidating.

I dial Leanne's number. I know they're no longer married, but Boone told me how much he cares for her, how much she means to him. They've already lost so much together. I figure it's only right she knows that he's in surgery right now.

When she picks up, she sounds confused. "Boone?" she asks. "I wasn't expecting to hear from you."

"This is actually Gray West, a friend of Boone's."

There's a pause. "Is everything okay?" she asks finally, probably realizing that it's unusual I'm on Boone's phone.

"No," I tell her, "it's not." I explain the events, and she lets out a long exhale.

"Oh my God. You've been through so much."

"Boone has too. It's been a long few days, but you can watch it all on the news."

"I'm turning it on right now," she says. "Wainwright!" she shouts, "put on Channel Four! I'm at the station," she tells me. "Oh wow," she says, "this is some Waco shit."

I bite my bottom lip. "Right, well, I just want to let you know that Boone's in surgery, and I'll let you know when he's out. I thought calling you was the right thing to do."

"I appreciate it," she says. "God, I had no idea the woman he was pining for was ..."

I press my lips together. How did she want to end this sentence? In a cult? A sister wife? The wife of a zealot? A woman married to a man twice her age who promised her eternal life?

I don't need her to finish the sentence. I'll let her think what she wants to think, but whatever her idea of me is, it's not the same as mine, because only I know what I've been through. Only I know what I've survived.

I tuck the phone away, pacing until someone calls out my name. A doctor enters the waiting room.

"Gray," he says, "your son, Abel, and Bethany are asking for you."

I stand, turning to Charlie. "You'll wait here?"

"Of course."

I follow the doctor to Bethany's room. Her eyes are closed, but when I enter the room, they flutter open.

"Hey," she says, softly. Abel holds her hand. My little boy has turned into a man.

"How are you holding up?" I ask them both.

Bethany licks her pink lips. She's always had the most angelic quality about her, soft and sweet. "I had a procedure," she says, "but I didn't feel anything." She blinks back tears and I step closer, giving her a hug. "I just really wanted our baby. But our baby is gone," she sobs.

"Oh, sweetheart," I say. "I'm so sorry." I sit down next to Abel, wrapping an arm around him. "You were so brave today," I tell him. "You're so strong."

He shakes his head. "No, Mom, you were. It's crazy, Dad always told us that women were the lesser gender, the weaker sex." He shakes his head. "But today you were so tough."

"I killed your father," I say, the words still so shocking.

"Yeah, but you saved everybody else."

"Would you mind if we called your sisters?" I ask. "They're out of school, and I know they miss us."

"Of course," he says.

I pull out the phone and dial Luna's number, making sure to press FaceTime this time. Luna calls for the girls right away, and when they see me, their smiles light up the screen. The moment they see their brother's face, they squeal. "Abel! Mom found you! Are you coming home?"

He looks over at Bethany. She starts crying softly. "Yeah, I'm coming home as soon as I can." Bethany's mother doesn't want her daughter coming home with us. She made that clear to me while I was with the police officers at the farmhouse. As soon as she is released from questioning, she plans on coming here to the hospital for her daughter.

"And Mom too, right?" Ruthie asks.

I smile. "Of course. I'll be home just as soon as I can. Maybe even tomorrow. We just had a little bit of a hiccup, and we're going to stay one more night. Okay?"

"Okay. We miss you," Ruthie says. "So much, Mama."

"I know, sweetheart. I miss you too."

"We still get a sleepover when you get home, right?" Olive asks.

"That was my promise," I say. "Pancakes for dinner."

Abel smiles. "You hate breakfast for dinner."

I laugh. My kids know me so well.

"Bethany gets to live with us too?" Olive asks.

"Maybe," I say. "We're going to have to sort

all that out, but we'll be home tomorrow. I promise."

We end the call, but it doesn't feel like anything's ended.

It feels like for the first time in forever, our story has just begun.

26

WE'VE BEEN BACK HOME at 212 Pinecrest Point for two weeks, and still, nothing feels normal. Abel is angry; Olive is moody, and Ruthie is clingy.

It's difficult knowing when to push, when to pull back, when to give in, and when to draw a line. I just want my children to be happy. And I feel a weight to every choice I make.

"You have to go to school," I tell Abel. "It's non-negotiable." It's Sunday night, and he is set to have his first day at the high school in the morning.

"I don't want to go if Bethany isn't with me," he says.

"I know, but I can't control Bethany's

mother. Tabitha is making the choices for her kids. Not me." I exhale, lifting the whistling kettle from the stovetop and pouring the hot water into my mug of chamomile tea. "And she'll be here next weekend to visit. That's something to look forward to."

He scoffs, rolling his eyes as he walks out of the kitchen.

The death of Garden Temple's prophet has meant the entire congregation is clinging to a new idea of what moving on means. It didn't help that since Jeremiah evaded the IRS for twenty years, the compound is completely closed until the investigation is over. The entire place is swarming with FBI agents, from what I've heard.

In the meantime, everyone has had to try and salvage a life for themselves somewhere else.

Naomi moved to Spokane with the help of Tracy and Tony. Lydia, who had her stomach pumped, miraculously survived her poisoning. She was able to move in with her mother, and her children are with her, though under the close eye of Child Protective Services.

Many members of the fold slipped out of the public eye quickly. Of course, Abel and

Bethany didn't want to part ways. And though I offered Bethany's mother Tabitha room at our home, she has a cousin she wanted to stay with just outside of Portland. I understand, but Abel doesn't see it the same way.

Thankfully, there's a compromise. Tabitha is letting Bethany take a train up to visit next weekend.

"Why is Abel so mad?" Olive asks, joining me in the kitchen.

"School starts tomorrow. And he misses Bethany." I grab another mug and make her some tea as well, handing it to her as we both move to the couch in the living room. Ruthie is sitting with a chapter book in her lap. Her hair is still damp from her after-dinner bath.

"He should be happy to go to school," Olive says. "I sure am."

Ruthie lifts her eyes from the page. "That's because Tomas is there."

"That isn't true!" Olive huffs.

"Yes, it is. You L-O-V-E him."

"I like school for lots of reasons, and it's dumb to boil it down to a boy. Grow up, Ruthie!"

"Hey," I say, reaching for Olive's arm, patting it. "Be gentle."

Her cheeks flush. And I know she is embarrassed for her outburst.

"Sorry, Olive," Ruthie says, pushing out her bottom lip. "I shouldn't tease."

Just then, there's a knock on the front door.

"It's Boone," Olive says, forgetting her sisterly dispute as she walks to the door and pulls it open to greet her favorite detective in the whole world.

"Hey, girls," he says, smiling at my daughters. His eyes land on mine and he grins. "I brought ice cream bars for the movie."

"Perfect," I say, standing to greet him, careful not to press hard against his arm that is in a sling. He is making a good recovery, and thankfully the bullet that he took didn't hit him anywhere detrimental.

He gives me a kiss on the cheek, and I have to step away from him in order to restrain myself. Truth is, I want to lean in close, let him hold me, never let go.

"How was your first physical therapy appointment?" I ask.

"Painful," he chuckles. "I feel like I've been through battle."

I smile softly. "I think we all have." I take the dessert from his hands and tell Olive to go get her brother.

"Time for movie night!" she shouts up the stairs.

"I said tell him, not scream at him," I say, shaking my head.

Boone is already on the couch next to Ruthie, asking about the book in her hands. Olive and Abel begin arguing over what movie to stream, and I smile to myself, feeling like this house is more of a home than ever. There are lots of wrinkles to iron out, but nothing we can't smooth in time.

My phone rings as I set the ice cream in the freezer. "Hello?"

"Hey, Gray," Charlie says. "You have a minute?"

"Sure, what's up?" We've spoken a handful of times over the last few weeks, and she has met me for coffee twice.

"I have some unsettling news and wanted to call right away."

"Should I be worried?" I laugh tightly.

"Well ... you know how when Ruthie was abducted, you and the kids all gave samples of DNA?"

"I remember."

"Well, they are all in our database now. And, well"—she clears her throat—"there's a DNA match you might be interested in."

"What do you mean?" I ask, my heart rate increasing.

Boone must wonder where I went off to because he joins me in the kitchen, mouthing a question, "Everything okay?"

I shake my head, turning on speakerphone and setting my phone on the counter.

"Do you have a daughter you placed in foster care fourteen years ago?" Charlie asks.

"A daughter?" I ask, shaking my head. Boone's eyes, though, lock with mine. My mind is racing to catch up with my heart.

A daughter.

"There is a girl named Esther Temple in our system, Gray. Do you—"

I gasp. "She died," I whisper. "She was two days old and—"

"She isn't dead," Charlie says. "She was placed into care as an infant, and since she had severe medical needs at the time, wasn't adopted. She has been in foster care her entire life."

The room spins, and I cover my mouth, horrified.

Jeremiah lied. I was in pain, suffering after I gave birth. All those years ago. He said Esther was weak, that she came too early.

And she did. She was five pounds, maybe less. So small, and I was a child myself, with a crying one-year-old and a husband who was angry over the idea that the baby might not be his.

That she could be Micah's.

She was struggling to breathe. Jeremiah said he took her to the hospital, but it was too late—she couldn't be saved. And I believed him.

Because my entire life was built around Jeremiah's words being holy.

He wouldn't lie. He was our prophet.

But he did.

Esther has been alive all these years.

Boone frowns. "But ... why is her DNA in the police database?" The question didn't come to my mind, but he's right to ask it.

"That's the thing that makes this complicated," Charlie says. "Esther has been charged with—"

"Charged?" I repeat, confused.

"Yes," Charlie says. "Your daughter has been charged with the murder of her foster father."

COMING FALL 2021:

THE SISTER WIFE'S DAUGHTER

SIGN UP FOR UPDATES ABOUT ANYA MORA'S
UPCOMING RELEASE:

HTTPS://ANYAMORA.COM/NEWSLETTER/

ALSO BY:

THE WIFE LIE

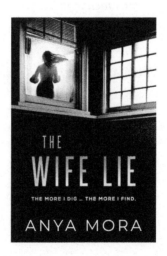

My husband is missing.
And his wife is on my doorstep.
The wife I never knew he had.

Does that mean my husband's out looking for
wife number three?

The more I dig... the more I find.

Ledger Stone is not the man I thought I knew.

What I'd thought was a whirlwind romance has
turned out to be a hurricane laced with lies.

It started with one.

Will it end with another?

*The Wife Lie is a domestic suspense novel where
secrets are buried deep.*

*Penny Stone gave up everything for the husband
she thought she knew -- and now she must uncover
the truth: just how much of her marriage was a lie?
And is their love worth fighting for?*

DOWNLOAD NOW: On Amazon

TUESDAY'S CHILD

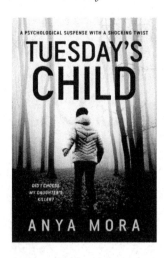

My daughter is dead.
My husband and I cling to what's left of our
family, desperate to make sense of the tragedy.
But when the sheriff knocks, he delivers news
no mother should ever have to hear.
Our daughter was murdered.
And my son is the prime suspect.

When we adopted eleven-year-old Holden, we
weren't wearing rose-colored glasses.
But we never could have imagined this.

They say you can't pick your family.
But I picked mine.
Did I choose my daughter's murderer?

Tuesday's Child is a gripping domestic

suspense. Doubt, desire, and the demise of a once picture-perfect family force Emery, wife to a state senator, to live out a mother's worst nightmare.

DOWNLOAD NOW: *On Amazon*

SECRETS MOTHERS KEEP

On Friday night in the clay fields of Bethel Creek, seventeen-year-old Daniel Reyes is found brutally attacked and left for dead.
On Saturday morning, Cora Maxwell finds her teenage son's clothes covered in blood.
A small town torn apart by a horrific hate crime.
An investigative reporter hell bent on finding the truth.

A mother's worst nightmare.
What really happened to the Reyes boy?

In the heart-stopping and timely suspense novel, Secrets Mothers Keep, widow and mother Cora Maxwell faces the hardest decision of her life.
In a world where there are few second chances, do you grant one to your child?
And if so... what is the cost?

DOWNLOAD NOW: *On Amazon*

ABOUT THE AUTHOR

Anya Mora lives in the Pacific Northwest with her family. Her novels, while leaning toward the dark, ultimately reflect light, courage, and her innate belief that love rewards the brave.

To learn about sales and new releases, sign up for Mora's mailing list here: https://anyamora.com/newsletter/

Made in the USA
Las Vegas, NV
17 October 2021